Kiss the Wallflower, book 6

COPYRIGHT

To Kiss a Highland Rose
Kiss the Wallflower, Book 6
Copyright © 2020 by Tamara Gill
Cover Art by Wicked Smart Designs
Editor Grace Bradley Editing
All rights reserved.

This book is a work of fiction. The names, characters, places, and incidents are products of the writer's imagination or have been used fictitiously and are not to be construed as real. Any resemblance to persons, living or dead, actual events, locales or organizations is entirely coincidental.

All rights reserved. Without limiting the rights under copyright reserved above, no part of this publication may be reproduced, stored in or introduced into a database and retrieval system or transmitted in any form or any means (electronic, mechanical, photocopying, recording or otherwise) without the prior written permission of both the owner of copyright and the above publishers.

ISBN: 978-0-6450581-2-3

DEDICATION

For my husbands Nanna, Dawn.

CHAPTER 1

Edinburgh – 1810

The first week of the Scottish Season was a crush and wonderful all at the same time. Lady Elizabeth Mackintosh admitted that being back within Scotland's society's bosom with all the scandalous goings-on was just what she needed. It had been two years since she'd traveled away from her brother's estate, taking part in the gaiety with her friends. Two women she loved dearly and who were forever reminding her of what she was missing. With a bountiful glass of chilled champagne in her hand, she inwardly toasted her unmarried friend, Lady Julia Tarrant, for making her attend tonight. The weeks to come were sure to be filled with laughter, fun, and perhaps marriage, if she were lucky enough to find a suitable husband.

God knows, she was well and truly old enough to find one.

The sound of a minuet filled the room, a collective murmur of gasps and chatter as couples made their way out onto the floor. Elizabeth watched the throng of guests, one of them her good friend, Lady Georgina Dalton, a widow, who seemed exceedingly happy with the man holding her in his arms and moving her through the steps of the dance. He was dashing, rakish even, if the wicked gleam in the gentleman's eyes was any indication.

Married twice and sadly widowed the same number, Georgina would have to be congratulated on having another man fall at her feet and so early in the Season. Now, if only introductions could be made for her with a suitable gentleman who piqued her interest, the night would be perfect indeed.

"Well, well, well, would ye look at that fine specimen of a gentleman? Too delicious to be English, dinna ye not think?" said her friend Julia, her gaze fixed on the man across the room.

Elizabeth laughed, taking her arm. Julia, Georgina, and Elizabeth had their Season in London the same year and had formed a close bond ever since. Of course, this was helped by the fact they were all Scottish by birth, heiresses, or had inherited their family's estates.

"Georgina certainly seems smitten by him. He's too dark-haired to be Scottish. Maybe Spanish, he certainly has eyelashes long enough to be European."

Julia nodded slowly. "Yes, and everyone knows a person's nationality can be guessed by how long one's eyelashes are," she teased.

Elizabeth grinned, not missing the sarcasm in her friend's tone. "Of course they can, silly. Did ye not know?" The gentleman in question glanced their way, and Elizabeth quickly looked elsewhere, not wanting to be caught ogling him like a debutante. But what were friends to do when one was dancing with such a dashing gentleman? One must look and admire.

Julia sighed. "Well, it seems the Spanish fox has caught his hare for the evening, and ye must agree, Georgina does seem taken with the gentleman."

"Ye said Georgina was very taken with another such gentleman last evening. I no longer hold any sway with yer words. You're a terrible tease." Elizabeth smiled, taking a sip of her champagne. "And what about you? Is there no one here tonight that has caught yer attention? Ye cannot remain unmarried forever. There must be a man somewhere in Scotland who's perfect for our Julia."

"No one here, I'm afraid, who is exciting enough to marry, but the Season is young and there are many more nights before us. Perhaps my luck may change. And let's not forget, my aunts have threatened to travel here should I not become betrothed before returning home, so I must find someone. If at all possible, I would prefer someone ancient, who'll pass away within the first year of marriage, and I'll not have to bother with husbands after that."

Elizabeth laughed, having forgotten Julia was constantly trying to calm and beguile her two aging aunts. They thought their charge needed their help in all things, including gaining a husband. "So true. I shall look about and see who's elderly enough to be suitable."

They both were quiet for a moment, watching the play of guests, when a pricking of awareness slid down Elizabeth's back. She gazed about the room, wondering what it was that had a shiver steal over her. "Should we move away from the windows? I think there's a draft here."

Julia nodded, and taking Elizabeth's arm, they headed to the opposite side of the ballroom. After a few moments at their new locale, the sense that someone was watching her wouldn't abate.

A gentleman bowed before them and asked Julia to dance. Her friend agreed, casting a grin over her shoulder as she walked off.

"Good evening, Lady Elizabeth."

The deep, English baritone sent a kaleidoscope of emotions to soar through her. Without looking at his face, she knew the man would be devilishly handsome, could curl her toes in her silk slippers.

"Do I know ye, my lord? I do not believe we've been introduced."

"That's because we have not. I'm Sebastian Denholm, Lord Hastings. It's a pleasure to have your acquaintance, my lady," he said, bowing before her with more deference than was needed.

The English earl everyone one was talking about this Season here in Edinburgh. A rakehell from London, rumored to be carousing in Scotland for new skirts to lift. Or so it was said.

"And ye know who I am? How is that so, my lord?"

He leaned conspiringly close. "Doesn't everyone know who you are?"

Elizabeth started at his reply, knowing too well what he hinted. It was no secret in the society they graced that she was known to be unlucky in love. Two years ago, she had set off for London to enjoy another Season. Her brother happily settled, she had stupidly thought she too might find such companionship.

How wrong she had been. In London, one by one, her friends had married around her. They were courted and whisked down the aisle before she had time to change her gown. Not her, however. She had been the good-luck charm for those looking to wed. Lucky Lizzie people started to term her.

Unlucky more like.

"I beg yer pardon, but I do not understand yer meaning." She would not let him throw her disastrous past Season in her face. No matter how handsome he may be.

"I remember you from town. London deemed you a good-luck charm for debutantes looking to marry. I see you have not been caught by such inducement yet, my lady."

Heat suffused her face. So he had heard of her. She'd fought hard to forget the many young women who befriended her so they could find husbands. It was the oddest situation and one reason she was attending this year's Season in Scotland. Even so, it did not look like she could escape those who attended from southern locales and who remembered. "How gentlemanly of ye to remind me of the title. Is that why you're speaking to me now? Do you hope that your nearness to me will equate to ye falling in love and marrying?"

He grinned down at her. "On the contrary. I have no interest in marriage to any of these chits."

Elizabeth fought to close her mouth, sure she was gaping at him. Did he mean that being by her rendered him safe? Was she so inept at finding a husband that the *gentlemen* now thought her a secure woman to be around, so long as other women did not hover close by? How absurd! Not to mention humiliating.

She turned, facing him. "Let me assure ye, my lord, that being by me does not make ye safe from marriage. I'm sure since I'm Lucky Lizzie, the charm would also work on the men who flock to my side. Ye would be no different."

"Do many men flock to your side, my lady? Or am I the only one?"

She narrowed her eyes on him, unsure where his questions were leading, if at all anywhere. Why was he near her if he was not interested? He seemed to be playing with words and her to an extent. She did not like it. "Ye are beside me, are ye not? I'm certain you will not be the last to grace my side this evening."

"I sought you out not to tease you, my lady, and I do apologize for bringing up your London Season. I merely wished to introduce myself and inform you of some news that I'm sure you will be well aware of soon enough."

"Really? What is this news ye wish for me to know?" Vaguely she remembered his lordship from town, a rake who enjoyed the *demimonde* and widows more than the debutantes. Handsome as sin, rich and wealthy like many of her acquaintance, but always the same. Men who looked for the next thrill, the next piece of skirt they could hoist. Not marriageable by any length. No matter what anyone said, rakes did not make the best husbands.

"You inherited Halligale, I understand."

"I did," she replied, saying nothing further. Her brother had gifted it not long after his marriage to Miss Sophie Grant. He had wanted her to have a home close to him, but that was hers. That it came with an abundance of land was equally generous. Her brother was simply the best person she knew.

"So, we're neighbors. I'm at Bragdon Manor," he continued.

She stared at him a moment, having not known that. If Lord Hastings was a Bragdon, he was closer to her than her brother was at Moy Castle. "I did not know ye had inherited."

Pain crossed his lordship's face, and the teasing light dimmed in his eyes. "I inherited the estate after my brother passed two years ago."

"I'm sorry for yer loss," she said, automatically reaching out and touching his arm. The moment she did, she knew it for the mistake it was. Shock rippled up her arm, a bolt of some kind she'd never experienced before. Elizabeth stepped back, breaking her hold.

"Thank you. My brother was a good man, if not ruled by vices that others sought to their advantage." His lordship seemed to shake off his melancholy and turned, watching her. He had dark eyes, almost gray, the blue so stormy. A handsome man and one who knew that fact well.

"We shall see each other often then," she said, sipping her champagne and willing her heart to stop beating fast in her chest. He was merely a man. A gentleman like no other. There was no reason her stomach would be all aflutter with him at her side.

He picked up her hand, kissing her gloved fingers. His eyes held hers, and again her skin prickled in awareness.

Oh, dear.

"I have traveled from England, Lady Elizabeth. I intend to see you as much as you will allow." With a wicked grin, he turned and strode off into the throng of guests, leaving her to watch him. Her gaze slid over his back before dipping lower. Well, it was not merely his eyes that were handsome, and what did he mean by his words? For the first time since her debut ball, excitement fluttered in her soul. Finally, perhaps this year, she would find love and have a marriage as strong and as sweet as her brother had found.

Maybe rakes did make the best husbands after all.

Sebastian headed toward the card room to seek out his closest friend Rawden, Lord Bridgman, who'd accompanied him to Scotland. Bridgman had readily agreed to travel north, as the timing suited him perfectly well since he also had some business to attend while in the country.

He found Rawden just as he was leaving a game of Loo and looking mightily pleased with himself.

"How was your evening, my good friend? I saw you speaking to Lady Elizabeth Mackintosh. Did she confirm what you suspected, that she has indeed inherited Halligale?"

Sebastian looked back to where he'd left Lady Elizabeth, but could no longer locate her in the crowd. "Yes, I spoke to her, and unfortunately, she has inherited the estate. I need to find a way to make her sell it back to me, or I suppose I could always take Laird Mackintosh to court and fight him over his unlawful acquiring of the lands."

Rawden raised his brow disbelievingly. "That would be a feat made for giants. He's Scottish, and the land is in Scotland. If you think the Scots will find the acquiring of Halligale unlawful, you have rocks in your head. You'd be best to marry the chit and acquire it back that way."

The comment from Rawden was off the cuff, meant as a lark, but Sebastian stilled, thinking over the fact. If he married her, he would get back his ancestral Scottish estate that had been in his family for hundreds of years. That his brother, the dead lout, had lost in a game of cards. It would be nothing but a mere inconvenience to him should he marry the woman who now owned it. She could stay in Scotland, and he could return to England, visiting Halligale whenever he chose. The idea had merit.

"She is handsome and seems to have wit. Maybe I will court her."

Rawden shrugged, taking two glasses of wine from a passing servant before handing him one. "To be married, though. I'm not sure you're ready for such a step. And anyway, I thought you liked the widow Lady Clifford. You were certainly cozy with her at her mask in London, which I may remind you everyone noted."

Sebastian groaned, knowing what a colossal mistake that had been. He'd been so far in his cups he'd not known what the hell he was doing. One moment he was dancing with Maria, and the next, he had her in a shadowed corner with his hands in places they ought not to be.

"Do not remind me of my past mistakes."

"So, I should not remind you then that she's here and

heading your way?" Rawden sipped his drink, laughter in his eyes.

Sebastian whirled about, panic seizing him. Maria was here! He took in the guests, only to see no one at all. Rawden laughed, doubling over, and Sebastian had the ultimate urge to kick him up the ass. "You think that is amusing. You're a bastard."

Rawden wiped at his eyes, laughing still and causing a bit of a spectacle of them. "I'm sorry, my friend. I could not help myself."

"Hmm," Sebastian said, sipping his drink and glancing yet again across the sea of heads to ensure Lady Clifford was not, in fact, in Scotland and could not get him in her clasp yet again.

"Lady Elizabeth is handsome, I will give her that. Do not be too hard on the chit. She probably does not know her brother won the estate in a game of cards."

"I never intended to be hard on her, but marrying her would certainly be cheaper than suing Mackintosh, and would be more pleasant for everyone. Why make war when you can make love with a woman like her?" He caught her moving through the guests, talking with another lady. Lady Elizabeth was tall, curved in all the right places, and with a bosom that would fit in his hands quite nicely. A well-developed lady, not some gangly, giggling debutante with no padding on her bones. Much more satisfying on one's palate.

Her laugh when it carried to him was carefree and without caution, bountiful and heartfelt. He liked the sound of it, and seducing her, marrying her, could make his few weeks in Scotland much more pleasant. Her brother may not like his sister's turn of events. Sebastian and Laird Mackintosh had already had terse words through correspondence over his acquiring of Halligale, but then, if his sister was in love, married even, what could Laird Mackintosh do about it?

Nothing.

"I'm glad to hear it," Rawden said, downing his drink. "Now, where are we off to next? Edinburgh is much like London. There is more than one ball a night to attend."

Sebastian laughed and started toward the house's foyer, all for experiencing what this ancient city had to offer that London did not. "Yes, of course, we have invitations for two other events this evening." And many more ladies to meet and flatter before he settled down to court Lady Elizabeth. With any luck, none of them would have emerald eyes and hair that blazed with a fire as bright as the sun itself.

CHAPTER 2

"You're killing the flowers, my dear. Please, move away before the roses become headless along with leafless." Julia stated, walking past, before slumping onto the settee and throwing her an amused glance.

Elizabeth sighed, glancing down at the roses she had been arranging. Her friend was right, the floral arrangement was well on the way to being atrocious. "We're for the Fishers' ball this evening, are we not?" she asked, sitting opposite Julia and giving up on her arrangement. The maids would do a better job in any case, she had no touch for decoration.

"We certainly are." Julia crossed her legs and met her gaze. "Are you still attending this evening? Or are you asking me about the ball as a means of telling me you've changed your mind?"

"Oh no, I'll be attending. I ran into Miss Wilson in the milliners this morning and she was all aflutter over Lord Hastings and his friend Lord Bridgman, who have arrived in Edinburgh for the Season it would seem. When I told Mrs. Wilson I had met Lord Hastings at the ball the other evening, she was beyond excitable and exclaiming that I must introduce his lordship to Emily. I do believe poor Emily was quite embarrassed by the whole conversation."

"I saw you talking with Lord Hastings the other evening. What did you think of the gentleman? His lordship and his friend, Rawden his name is rumored to be, are both too handsome for their own good."

Heat stole up Elizabeth's cheeks thinking of Lord Hastings' last words to her. That he wished to see her often. "He was very polite and kind. His downfall is that he's English, but since I have had an English sister-in-law these past few years, I have become used to their ways and I do not find them so very different to us."

Julia scoffed. "You make the English sound like they come from another planet!" She laughed.

Elizabeth chuckled. "Well, they almost do, do they not?"

Julia sighed, leaning back into the settee. "You're young and healthy, an heiress with an estate all your own. Lord Hastings would be lucky indeed if he captured your love. But the Season is young and there are many such gentleman as he. Do not set your cap on him too soon, cast your eye across everyone who's traveled north and decide if anyone else may suit you better."

Elizabeth raised her brow. Her friend had a point and she was right. The Season was young and there were many more balls to enjoy yet. "You know you're starting to sound quite intelligent. I think I shall do as you say."

Her friend smiled triumphally. "How many years have I been telling you so, but you have not believed me? If you follow my advice, you shall never go astray. And if Lord Hastings is genuinely interested in ye, he will not be put off should ye dance or be played court to by others. He will simply be all the more determined."

The idea of his lordship being determined to win her

made her feel all tingly and excited. His dark, hooded eyes the other night she could happily fall into and never escape. So handsome, and that he had opted for a Scottish Season this year did say a lot about his intellect. He was obviously smart on that score. The London Season was overrated.

Julia picked up a cushion and held it atop her lap, playing with the multitude of tassels along its side. "What do ye make of Lord Bridgman? He's an interesting character, do ye not agree?"

Her friend's interest in the man was not missed and Elizabeth bit back a grin. "I dinna meet his lordship, but he seemed pleasant enough when I did spot him about the room. He certainly is what they say of him…handsome."

"I think I shall pursue him and see what comes of it. And if I keep his lordship occupied, it will enable you to get to know Lord Hastings better before ye make your choice." Julia grinned. "It is simply the perfect plan."

"It seems you have everything all worked out perfectly well, but I have not even decided if I want to seek his interest. You, however, may court Lord Bridgman if ye choose."

Julia held up her hands in defeat. "Very well, do as ye must, but I think ye should at least see if you suit. It is not often such a stunning pair of men enter our small society. We must make the most of it when we can."

The door swung open and in walked Georgina, a maid carrying a tray of tea and biscuits close on her heels.

"Good morning, my dears. I hope you all slept well."

At the benign question, something that Georgina was not known for, Elizabeth considered her friend. "What has happened, Georgina? It is not like you to care." She grinned, pouring herself a cup of tea.

"I've decided to hold a masquerade and you're both invited." Georgina picked up a biscuit, taking a generous bite.

"We live with you, Georgina. I think our invitation was always going to be delivered," Julia said, shaking her head.

"We shall invite everyone in Edinburgh for the Season, and it'll be the ball of the year. You may invite Lord Hastings, Elizabeth darling. He seemed quite taken with you the other evening."

She groaned. Julia choked on her tea, tried and failed miserably to mask it with a cough.

"I have just spent the last ten minutes explaining to Julia why I shall leave my options open. He spoke to me once. That does not mean he's the least interested in getting under my skirts."

Georgina grinned. "I do adore that I'm rubbing off on you, Elizabeth darling."

Elizabeth took a sip of tea, better that than to scream at her friend's teasing ways.

"You shall invite Lord Hastings, but please do not think there is anything between us. I spoke to him once." She took a calming breath, not wanting to discuss the Englishman anymore. Surely there were other more interesting subjects to talk about than him. Even if the memory of him was amusing and somewhat wicked with his parting words.

Georgina, sensing Elizabeth's annoyance, thankfully changed the subject. "Well, I had the most delightful dance with Lord Fairfax the other evening. He owns half of the Highlands. I think I may let him pursue me. Did you see him, girls? He was most handsome, was he not?"

Julia nodded, her eyes bright with excitement. "Oh yes, he was an interesting gentleman. He was certainly charmed by *your* charms, is what I noticed most."

Georgina threw a grape at Julia, who picked it up off her skirt and plopped it in her mouth. "I think I shall let him kiss me at the mask. I'm sure he will try."

"You have just come out of mourning. Do you really wish

for another husband so soon? If you marry before me yet again, I shall be forever termed the friend who cannot find a husband for herself. People will think that you being around me has enabled men to fall in love with you as they did in England. The good-luck love charm. I'll be mortified," Elizabeth declared, already hearing the whispers and tattle that would travel from Scotland all the way to Almacks in London.

"I promise ye, my dear, that I shall not marry again until you are safely in the arms of the man you'll love forever and a day. But that doesn't mean I cannot have restrained fun this Season. I'm a widow, after all. As long as I'm discreet," Georgina said, a wicked glint in her eyes.

"Well, I for one am going to enjoy my time here, as we all should. And we shall help ye in choosing a fine, sweet man who will love you as much as we love you, Elizabeth. He is out there, you know. And one can never say that Lord Hastings is not that man. If he seeks you out again, you must help him on with your regard. If he senses your interest, then you may be able to secure his affections."

Elizabeth slumped back in her chair, feeling drained and tired from all the work she had before her already, and it was still the first week of the Scottish Season. "My brother would skin me alive if he heard I was acting fast up in Edinburgh. With Sophie expecting, the last thing he needs is for a salacious rumor that his sister has turned rogue when it comes to finding a husband, and then traveling all the way up here to drag me home."

"He will do no such thing. He is too distracted to take any notice of what we're all up to in Edinburgh. The first he shall hear of anything will be your betrothal." Julia set down her cup and clapped her hands, gaining their attention. "Now, my dears, about this ball. What should the theme be, do ye think?"

"Well," Georgina said, "we could allow the guests to choose, but maybe notable characters throughout history. Thoughts?"

Julia nodded. "Oh yes, I shall go as Cleopatra."

"Heloise will do well for me. I'm as doomed in love as she is." Elizabeth was half-joking when she nominated her costume, even so, a small part of her reminded her that just because what all of London believed her to be before she left, a luck charm for her friends, but unlucky herself, did not make it true. This Season she could either let the past dictate her future or she could clasp the fun on offer here in the capital and enjoy herself to the fullest. Living with Georgina allowed more freedom than she'd ever had before. Her friend being a widow enabled her to act as a chaperone too. They could come and go as they pleased, sleep all day and dance all night if they wanted. What more could she ask for?

Julia and Georgina both barked out a laugh, their eyes brimming with unshed tears of mirth. "Oh my dear, you are not going as Heloise. I shall not allow it. No, you shall go as Peitho, the goddess of love and seduction, for that is who ye are and will be not just for this ball, but for the Season. No more lucky charm for others, my dear. It is time ye were the lucky charm for yourself."

Georgina grinned, nodding. "Peitho it is. Now, we must head down to the dressmaker and have her make our gowns. We must look the best since we're hosting. Oh, what fun we shall have."

"What hearts we shall steal," Julia continued.

"And what kisses we shall enjoy," Elizabeth finished, smiling and thinking that perhaps, this year, things would be different. She was with two women who were her true friends and had her back at every turn. They would not see her wronged and she would not be a wallflower this year, nor ever again.

CHAPTER 3

"If you stare at the doors any longer, people will start to think you are a simpleton."

Sebastian tore his gaze away from Sir Fisher's entrance and concentrated instead on the gathered throng of guests. To his surprise, there were many from London. Even a few ladies who had debuted last Season but would seem to not have found a match were present.

"I do not know why Lady Elizabeth is so late this evening. I cannot make her fall in love with me if she is not here." Sebastian said, his tone gruffer than it ought to be, considering Rawden was trying to stop him from looking like a besotted fool, which he was not. Far from it, no matter how tempting Lady Elizabeth was to the eye, she was a means to an end. His way of gaining back a family estate that should never have been lost.

"Your fascination with the doors was gathering interest, and we can't have that." Rawden chuckled, and Sebastian ground his teeth. "But never fear, my friend, the woman who shall be yours has arrived. How fortunate for you both."

Sebastian glared at Rawden, not missing the sarcasm in his tone before. As casually as he could muster, he cast his attention toward the doors. The breath in his lungs seized, his skin prickled. Never had he ever seen someone as beautiful as the woman London had dubbed Lucky Lizzie.

How had the men of his acquaintance not seen her beauty? He swallowed hard, tempering the desire that rose within him at the sight of her.

"What are your plans with Lady Elizabeth? How will you go about courting her without her hearing that your family once owned Halligale? If she hears such a thing, she will be suspicious of you. The chit does not come across as a simpleton that one can fool."

She was not. Even from the short time they had spent together at the last ball, Sebastian gathered such a truth. "I can only hope she does not. I will tell her, of course, one day, but not until we're wed."

Rawden threw him a disbelieving look. "You are very sure of your charms. What if she is not interested? What shall you do then?"

"There is nothing I can do." He shrugged, hoping that was not the case. He'd always been popular with the opposite sex, never went without when it came to pleasures of the flesh. He cast his eye back to where Lady Elizabeth and her friends made their way through the gathered guests, speaking to those they knew. No, she would be no different, and from the rosy blush that had crossed her features upon their introduction, she would be an easy conquest. "I'm certain she will not be troublesome."

Rawden chuckled, sipping his wine. "I disagree. I think she shall be harder to crack than you think. These Scottish lasses have sturdier backbones than our English flowers. You do know that their national flower is a Thistle. That should give you a little indication of their prickliness."

Sebastian choked on his wine, laughing at his friend's words. "I consider myself duly warned." He cleared his throat, watching Lady Elizabeth as they came to stand across from them in the room. Her gown was deep purple, almost black, and shimmered under the candlelight as if it had a fine, sheer fabric over the top of the silky material. The color set off her green eyes and pink, kissable lips. His body hummed with the thought of her in his arms. He loved the chase, and she was a worthy and desirable woman to catch.

"Before Lady Elizabeth catches you ogling her like the besotted fool, all but drooling down your chin, care for a game of cards? I have a desire to procure some good, Scottish blunt. The night is young, and you have time to court your lady later in the evening."

"Lead the way," Sebastian said, distracted somewhat by the popinjay leading Elizabeth out onto the dance floor. The fop was a short man, and barely came up to Elizabeth's chin. He would never do for such a striking woman. He narrowed his eyes. Surely that wasn't the type of gentleman Elizabeth wished to be coupled with for the remainder of her life.

Rawden clapped him on the shoulder and laughed. "Stop, Sebastian. You'll scare her away before you have a chance to win her."

Sebastian harrumphed, supposing that may be true.

They paused inside the card room doors, taking in the gentlemen who were already playing. A footman brought over a tray of whisky, the delectable amber liquid just what Sebastian needed.

"Oh, before I forget. I have news, and some I think you'll be pleased with."

"What is it?" Sebastian asked, taking a healthy swallow of his drink.

"This afternoon, we received an invitation from Lady Georgina Dalton to her masquerade ball. The woman your conquest is living with for the Season. There is one hitch. The ball is being held at Lady Dalton's home out of Edinburgh. The estate is quite large from all accounts, and she has opened her home for her guests to stay a day or two afterward if they wish before returning to town."

A mask? How fortunate for such a ball to be held. One always enjoyed such entertainments where they had an edge of secrecy—a place for clandestine rendezvous. "When is it?" he asked, hoping it was soon. The more time he had with Lady Elizabeth, the better his outcome in winning her would be.

"The week after next," Rawden replied.

Rawden gestured to a table that two gentlemen stood up from, leaving the remaining players short. "Care for a game of whist? Let us show these Scottish lads how real men play cards."

"After you," Sebastian said, not quite sure his friend had picked the worst-playing gentlemen in the room, the size of their winnings putting paid to that notion.

"I'll deal," Rawden declared, introducing them to the other two players.

Sebastian sat, played without much thought while his mind debated how to court Lady Elizabeth. He needed to come across as genuine in his regard. He'd never had to act a lovesick fool before, and it would be new, if not somewhat degrading, to do so. Even so, his marrying her was for the best. It meant that Halligale was once again in his family, to be inherited by the future Earls of Hastings.

It was an unfortunate necessity and one he would not fail at. The estate would not be long in Mackintosh hands. Not after this Season, at least.

𝓑y the time Elizabeth arrived at Georgina's estate for the masquerade ball, the preparations were in full swing. Maids ran from room to room, up and down stairs, setting up the ball and the guest rooms. The footmen looked frayed from their endless chores and orders. Standing in the foyer, she pulled off her gloves, not missing the unmistakable sound of Georgina emitting orders from the front parlor. Julia, who traveled with Elizabeth to the estate, rolled her eyes just as Georgina strode into the foyer.

"La, you're here." Georgina handed them both a piece of parchment, pointing at it. "Here are yer chores to do before the guests arrive tomorrow. Do let me know if ye have any questions."

Julia looked over the parchment. She frowned before scrunching up the note in her hand. "Georgina," she said, leading them toward a private sitting room across the hall from the library. "What possessed ye to be so stringent with everyone who's staying here? Ye cannot possibly think we want to do these activities in the short amount of time we're here. I think the ball is adequate enough to keep the guests occupied."

Georgina gaped at Julia as if she'd sprouted two heads.

Elizabeth quelled her smile. "Julia, you're mean. All Georgina wants to do is ensure everyone has a lovely time." She patted her friend's hand, noting Georgina had yet to find her voice.

Julia unfolded the scrunched-up list. "I cannot swim, and yet I'm supposed to be boating out on the loch. Are ye trying to kill your guests with drowning as well as boredom?"

"These suggestions were merely that, a suggestion. I only wanted my guests to know they have plenty of things to occupy their time here. I will not be out on the lawn each morning blowing a whistle and making ye all stand in line if that's what ye think."

Elizabeth grinned, imagining such a scene. "Of course, you won't be, and we never thought ye would. Julia's just in a mood because her aunts are on their way to watch her every move."

"I don't know why they have come. Georgina is a widow, adequate chaperonage for anyone."

Georgina stood and rang the bell for tea. "Not to mention my father has arrived to watch over all of us too. He's come back from London specially. I think he believes I'm still in pigtails." Georgina frowned. "Why did yer aunts insist on coming? They never have before."

Julia sighed. "To be nosy, I would imagine. They have heard the two Englishmen are going to be present and insisted they join the mask."

"I'm sure yer father can be persuaded to keep Julia's aunts occupied. They are of a similar age in any case," Elizabeth said.

"True," Georgina sat just as a knock sounded on the door before a footman brought in a tray of tea.

"Do ye really think people will have time for such games and diversions? They'll arrive, prepare for the ball the following day, and some will travel back to Edinburgh the day after. Must we prepare these events as well? We'll have enough to do with ensuring the ballroom, the food, and the house are ready for so many guests as it is," Julia pleaded.

"I just wanted options." Georgina looked down at her hands, a small frown between her brow.

"It is to yer credit that ye want everyone to have a wonderful time, and they will. The mask is going to be a major success, the ball of the Season. You do not need anything else pulling your guests from what they have traveled here to enjoy." Elizabeth reached out, patting Georgina's hands.

Julia sighed, coming over to sit beside Georgina. "I'm sorry, dearest, for being curt. I'm tired from my travels, that is all. If ye truly want yer guests to do other things at the estate, then we shall, of course, help ye prepare."

Georgina's lips lifted into a small smile. "It's quite alright. I can see that I've been overzealous with my planning. The ball is enough. You're quite right."

"Now, do tell us who else is to arrive." Elizabeth settled back in her chair, relieved that her friends were back to being polite to one another.

"Most of our acquaintances from town, the two Englishmen, of course," Georgina said, throwing a pointed stare at her. "Just about everyone we know, but the house is large enough, the staff has been run off their feet this past week. It's been bedlam here, or so I've been told."

"I cannot wait to dance. My costume of Cleopatra is simply divine," Julia said, pouring herself a cup of tea.

Elizabeth listened as her friends discussed their gowns, how they would do their hair, and who they wished to dance with. The mask was certain to be a success, a night of dancing, of mystery and intrigue. She had not attended a masked ball since her first Season in London, and it would be nice to have one here in Scotland.

The idea that this time tomorrow they would be preparing for a ball sent a thrill up her spine. That Lord Hastings would soon be here was a welcome thought. Would he ask her to dance? Or would he stride off yet again without a backward glance as he had done previously?

Would she dance with him if he did ask? She would, of course. If only to see if her heart fluttered in his presence. Or determine that it was merely an odd reaction toward him upon their first introduction.

Time would reveal all, she supposed, at the masked ball.

CHAPTER 4

*S*ebastian knocked Rawden's leg, smiled as his friend, whose face was squashed up against the carriage window, stuttered awake and wiped the dribble from his mouth. "I do so enjoy watching you wash the window with your own drool." He laughed as Rawden mumbled unintelligible words before sitting up and trying to wake.

"Are we here then? A ghastly long trip, was it not?"

"We're four hours from Edinburgh. I hardly think it's worthy of the word ghastly. And cheer up, Rawden, for we have arrived." The carriage lurched sideways as they passed through the gates of Lady Georgina's estate. Sebastian could see the house nestled in the valley below, small lines of smoke billowing from the numerous chimneys.

"I wonder if the prickly Lady Julia Tarrant will be there. It should make the ball more amusing with such women to spar with. Not to mention Lady Georgina is soft on the eyes."

Sebastian raised his brow. "Do behave. We do not need to be escorted off the property and sent back to the capital with our tails between our legs before I have a chance with Lady

Elizabeth. I have a property to get back. I can't have you causing any more trouble than I will myself should she find out my motives."

"I am your friend, and I support you in all that you do, but are you not the least bit unsettled by this plan? If you court her, win her heart, she will think you're genuine in your regard of her, which as much as you like her, possibly find her attractive, you will be marrying her for her land." Rawden fixed his cravat, and Sebastian turned to look back outside the carriage window, thinking on his friend's words. "Think of it this way," Rawden continued. "Had your brother not lost the estate, would you be in Scotland chasing Lady Elizabeth's skirts? I think not. You would have traveled up north for hunting and not much else."

Sebastian pushed away the guilt that pricked at his conscience. It may seem underhanded, ungentlemanly to court a woman for what she would bring to the marriage, but he had little choice. Halligale had been his home for a great deal of his childhood. Where his Scottish mother raised her two boys. Most of his fondest memories were swimming in the loch or running through the grounds, the heather, everything that made Scotland what it is. He loved the home, and so if he had to marry a woman he liked very much and not much else to gain it back, he would.

"First, shall I remind you that this was your idea? I had not thought of that option myself until you said so. But sleep soundly, I will treat Lady Elizabeth with respect. I shall not have a mistress, and she'll want for nothing. She never needs to know that our marriage was brought about by the estate she now owns."

The carriage rocked to a halt, and Sebastian waited for the footman, who hurried from the front steps to assist them alight.

He climbed down, looking up at the large castle that had

been built on to at some point. That Lady Georgina was accommodating some of the guests at her ball became perfectly clear. The house was well equipped to house many guests.

"Marvelous," Rawden said, coming to stand beside him. "If I was not so taken with Lady Tarrant, I may try for Lady Georgina instead if this is the home that she brings to the marriage."

Sebastian glared at Rawden and his comment that did not pass his notice.

A willowy figure exited the main doors to the house. Sebastian met the deep-green depths of Lady Elizabeth's eyes, his sole reason for attending. She was dressed in an afternoon gown, a lighter shade of her eyes. The small cardigan over her shoulders accentuated her bosom, and he was reminded of how well-endowed and pretty the woman was.

"Lady Elizabeth, how lovely to see you again." Sebastian came up to her, taking in her flushed cheeks. Did his arrival cause her pinked complexion? Perhaps his winning of her heart would be easier than he thought.

"And you, Lord Hastings," Elizabeth replied, smiling in welcome.

There was a rustle of skirts before Lady Georgina stepped outside, coming toward him and Rawden with outstretched hands.

"Welcome to Teebrook, Lord Hastings, Lord Bridgman. I hope yer journey north wasn't too tiring?"

"Not at all," Sebastian said, bowing over his hostess's hand. "I had good company, and so the time passed quickly. And we were eager to see your home and meet with you all again."

Georgina smiled, and Sebastian had to agree the woman was quite pretty, but not as pretty as Elizabeth. "Thank ye so much, we are looking forward to the ball also. I hope ye have an enjoyable stay here."

Sebastian stepped back and gestured to his friend, whose gaze was fixed on Lady Georgina. "May I present Lord Rawden Bridgman, second son to the Duke of Albury?"

"We're honored," she said, dipping into a perfect curtsy, laughter alighting her eyes. "Would you like a cup of tea, or perhaps you'd prefer to settle in before dinner this evening? Luncheon has been laid out in the breakfast room if you're hungry after your travels."

"If a servant could show us to our rooms, that would be preferable, I think. We'll come down soon and break our fast."

Georgina waved a footman over, and soon Sebastian and Rawden followed the man who carried his luggage inside. The foyer was monstrous, a double oak staircase leading to the first floor. Guests already arrived wished them good afternoon, smiling in welcome while going about the house. Paintings adorned the walls, rugs littered the floors, a means of keeping the house warm in winter, he supposed. Candles burned from the sconces and upon hallway furniture, keeping the darkened halls at bay. Rawden was deposited in a room first before the servant showed Sebastian to his.

The suite was generous. A large, four-poster bed with tartan curtains sat against a dark wood-paneled wall. A fire burned bright in the grate and a daybed sat just off to the side of it, along with a single chair in deep-green leather. The room evoked a masculine feel, and Sebastian thought it quite acceptable. What a shame they would not be here long.

"Would you like me to send up the manservant assigned to you to unpack, my lord?"

Sebastian nodded, walking to the windows and to the view that captured his attention. Halligale did not even have such a beautiful view. The start of the Highlands in the distance was certainly impressive.

"And hot water, if you please," he added when the servant went to leave. "I need to bathe."

"Of course, my lord."

Sebastian worked his cravat free, throwing it aside. He should have brought his valet, Wilson, but staying here two nights, he did not think it necessary. He would have the servant unpack his things and set everything out for tomorrow night's mask.

He had opted for no costume, preferring a black, superfine suit. He did, however, have a mask that covered up much of his face. The evening was set to be one the Edinburgh society would not forget, and he, for one, hoped it was one that Lady Elizabeth did not forget either.

After bathing, Sebastian fell promptly asleep, and it was only when the servant from earlier woke him for dinner did he realize how late it was. Dressing quickly and hearing the dinner gong sound deep in the house, Sebastian strode down the hall, looking forward to the evening ahead.

He fiddled with his waistcoat and did not hear the door to another room open or see the woman who barreled into him at a force that sent him reeling. His arms instinctively reached out to stop her from falling. It did not work, she propelled him back, and they both went down, the delectable, supple Lady Elizabeth's body finding its home atop his.

"In a hurry for dinner, my lady?" She scrambled off him, her eyes wide with horror.

"I do apologize, my lord." Elizabeth stood, adjusting her

gown, which he just now noticed. For dinner, she wore a deep, satin red, her lips glistening with a touch of rouge. The breath in his lungs seized, and for a moment, he merely stared at her. He knew she had red locks, but tonight, coiled up high, her fierce, green eyes and gown made her appear the most delectable Scottish lass he'd ever beheld.

Damn it, she is beautiful.

"I should have been watching where I was going. I'm normally quite punctual, and when I heard the dinner gong, and I wasn't already downstairs, I hurried. I am so sorry for not only running into ye, but…"

Sebastian waved her concerns aside as he dusted down his clothing. "It was my fault. I should have been paying attention to my steps ahead instead of adjusting my waistcoat."

She blushed prettily but nodded. "Of course. Shall we go downstairs together then?"

"It would be my pleasure." Their short walk to the dining room was not nearly long enough. Now that he was with Lady Elizabeth, he did not want to part from her or share her time with others. His courting required him to be with her, and preferably alone, or at least apart from the other guests.

How else would he ever get to kiss those delectable lips?

By the time they entered the dining room, the other guests were taking their seats. Sebastian led Lady Elizabeth to her chair, throwing her a small smile before moving on to where the hostess had him placed, which fortunately was directly beside her.

"How fortunate for us that we're to be dinner companions." Sebastian sat, placing a napkin across his knee.

Elizabeth smiled in agreement. "How are you finding Edinburgh? Are you enjoying our Season here in Scotland?"

"I am, very much so. Your company in particular." Sebastian held her gaze for longer than he should and was pleased to see her blush. Oh yes, she was already a little in love with him. It would be no chore to win her hand and his house at the same time.

*E*lizabeth turned her attention to the kale brose soup, rich with color, and smelling of vegetables and broth laid before her, wondering why Lord Hastings would say something so inappropriate. He enjoyed her company, that was all very well, but he should not have told her in such a forward manner. Whatever had come over the man?

While she did not mind his company, she was also wary. His particular attention did not make sense. She was known as Lucky Lizzie. Gaining husbands for others, somehow her gift. While he may think himself safe from her because he was male and not female, that did not ring true at all. Not if all the admiring glances directed at him were any indication.

She studied him as he took a sip from his wine, and her stomach fluttered anyway. He was awfully handsome. It was no surprise women flocked to him, that all of Edinburgh was aflutter with his presence in the city this year.

"I am most disappointed that I did not meet you when you were in London last. Promise me at tomorrow night's mask that you will save the waltz for me."

"Of course, if that is what ye wish. I have not been asked to save any dances yet, so I shall write your name on my dance card when I retire for the night." Elizabeth turned back to her meal. If she concentrated on the soup, the man beside her would surely be less diverting. The idea that he may be singling her out due to interest was not something she had considered before. She had been so unlucky in the past that she now automatically assumed no one would find her handsome.

That his lordship seemed genuine in his focus on her was

a welcome diversion. A pleasant change from how her Seasons had traveled in the past.

The tapping of a crystal glass caught her attention, and she looked up to see Georgina's father, Earl Cathcourt, standing at the head of the table and smiling down at everyone. He was a jovial-looking gentleman and known for his kindness toward others. "Ladies and gentlemen, let me welcome ye all to Teebrook. My daughter and I hope yer stay here is enjoyable and memorable too."

The ladies about the table smiled in sweet agreement while the men nodded. It amused Elizabeth to note that the two women most interested in Lord Cathcourt's words were Julia's elderly aunts. Maybe Georgina's father would be able to distract the sisters for the ball's duration and allow Julia to enjoy herself without chastisement.

"Georgina." The earl gestured to his daughter. "You wished to say a few words."

"I did. Thank ye, father." Georgina stood. "I too wished to welcome ye and thank ye for traveling here at such short notice. The masked ball is sure to be a magical evening, and we hope you all enjoy your short stay here. After dinner this evening, there will be music, cards, and if anyone is inclined, dancing in the green drawing room, which for those who have not toured the house as yet, is the original castle's great hall."

A muffled, excited chatter sounded about the table, and Elizabeth had to admit the short house party here was exciting, made one almost not want to return to Edinburgh.

"I hope you all have a lovely stay and will come back to see us all very soon." Georgina sat, smiling at the guests.

Lord Cathcourt raised his glass in toast of his daughter's speech. Elizabeth raised hers, turned to see Lord Hastings watching her, a small smile playing about his mouth.

"To masked balls, my lady," he said, tapping his glass against hers.

"Of course," Elizabeth replied, unsure how to react to a man who looked at her as if he would like to devour her, just as a wolf would a rabbit. This being courted was a whole new experience for her. When in London, she supposed her Scottishness had gone against her. With fiery red hair and freckles across her nose, she was under no illusion she was not as perfect as the English liked their ladies. She was a little rough about the edges, opinionated, and her hair often did whatever it wished. Did Lord Hastings not mind her quirks? How diverting if he did not.

How alluring.

CHAPTER 5

*E*lizabeth, along with Julia and Georgina, came downstairs and walked through the ballroom before the other guests were due to arrive. Many of those in attendance stayed at the castle, while some from nearby properties would come within the hour.

The room was everything one could wish for a masked ball. Seductive, secretive, and decadent. Hundreds of tallow candles burned in the chandeliers above their heads. Flowers and sheer, black fabric looped across the ceiling, making the room appear smaller and more wicked to the eye. Some of the large, porcelain sculptures were brought in to give the appearance of grandeur, miniature crowns placed atop their heads to mark them as royal statues.

There was gold everywhere, and in the short amount of time that Georgina had to prepare for this ball, Elizabeth wasn't sure how she had been able to pull it off so well, but she had. The space was magnificent. The orchestra too was dressed in black-and-gold livery, as well as the footmen serving at the ball.

"This is amazing, Georgina. Tonight is certainly going to

be the place to be and talked about for the remainder of the Season." Elizabeth clasped Georgina's hands, squeezing them. "How clever ye are."

Julia smiled, turning in a circle to take it all in. "I'm in awe, truly. Tonight is going to be so pleasurable. I can hardly wait."

"I'm glad ye like it," Georgina said, walking toward the orchestra and telling them that they may commence. "I wanted it to be magical, and I think I have succeeded." She turned back to them. "Ye both look striking. Lord Hastings and Lord Bridgman will not know what has hit them when they see ye two."

Julie blushed, and Elizabeth glanced down at her gown. As her friends had decreed, she was dressed as Peitho, the goddess of love and seduction. The robes she wore were certainly seductive, and when she'd first viewed the gown, a shiver of caution had run through her at how risqué it appeared.

Her face was covered with a golden mask, disguised with paste diamonds. Elizabeth had painted her lips a deep red, and for the first time in all her life, she did not feel herself. The gown of black-and-gold silk left her feeling bold and seductive, just like the goddess, she supposed.

Georgiana joined her father as he entered the room and took their places near the door to welcome the guests who had started to trickle in. Elizabeth and Julia moved over by the terrace doors, pushed wide this evening to allow the guests to stroll on the terrace and gardens beyond.

"You look beautiful, Julia. Do you think you shall know Lord Bridgman when he arrives? For all that you deny the insinuation, I know that you like him."

Julia smiled, her eyes twinkling behind her black mask. "I do like him, and I like teasing him even more. I think I shall know him. He let it slip that he's coming as King Henry the

8th. The robes themselves, Tudor in design, will give him away if his features do not."

"Do you think there may be something between you beyond the Scottish Season?" Elizabeth asked, curious at her friend's thoughts. Julia was more private than she and Georgina were, not with her opinions, but certainly regarding her thoughts on love.

"Perhaps," she said, shrugging. "We shall have to see if Lord Bridgman's kisses are as wicked as his words have been. Until then, I will not make a decision."

Elizabeth chuckled, sipping her champagne. "I like Lord Hastings, more than I thought I would like an Englishman. The way he looks at me sometimes." Her heart beat fast at the memory of the look in his eye at last night's dinner. Determined came to mind, along with want. "I think I should like to kiss him too to decide on his suitability to me."

Julia laughed as more people flocked into the room. They spoke to anyone who came over to them, wishing them a pleasant evening, and it wasn't before too long the room was bursting at the seams with guests. The dancing had commenced, and the loud hum of conversations rent it almost impossible to hear each other speak.

The thought of seeing Lord Hastings again made nerves skitter across her skin. No man had ever made her feel such emotion, and while she liked the idea of his flirting with her, she could not help but worry that it wasn't genuine. She had been so unlucky in the past for herself that she could not shake the fear that it would be the same with his lordship. That another woman would waltz by and take his attention, and she would be forgotten in the crowd.

"Lord Hastings is headed this way, Elizabeth. I think that is him over by the Grecian statue." Julia nodded in the direction she meant, and Elizabeth turned to see if she was correct.

The breath in her lungs seized. Her mind scrambled for words. He was dressed in classic black, a long, dark domino over his shoulders and a mask covering half his face, leaving half his lips and one eye visible.

He swooped into a bow before them, a teasing grin on his lips. "Lady Elizabeth, Lady Julia, you both look remarkably beautiful." His lordship turned to Elizabeth, his attention stealing over every part of her like a physical caress. She breathed deep, scrambling to regain her wits.

What on earth was wrong with her? Was she so desperate for a husband that she saw interest where there was no interest to be seen? Dear heavens, how pitiful if that were true.

"I hope you have not forgotten our dance, my lady." He clasped her hand, kissing the top of her gold silk gloves. His eyes meeting hers as his lips touched.

"I have not forgotten, my lord," she managed, ignoring the nervous wabble in her voice.

He smiled and came to stand beside her. Lord Bridgman was not far behind his friend, and he soon swooped Julia into his arms and out onto the dance floor for a Scottish reel.

"I knew it was you the moment I came into the room. I think I could pick you out of a crowd anywhere."

Elizabeth chuckled, shaking her head. "Really, my lord? Is my costume so very bad to pick me out of a crowd so easily?"

He reached out, picking up a loose curl and sliding it through his fingers. Her heart stilled, her mind imagining his hands caressing other parts of her just so.

"Your hair, you see. Such a beautiful, rich red, makes one want to run their fingers through it to see if it singes one's skin."

Elizabeth couldn't form words. No one had ever said her hair was lovely. And yet the way Lord Hastings was looking at her right at this moment, she could almost believe he was earnest.

"You're in Scotland. There are many of us with such colored hair. I think you're flirting with me, my lord." And she loved that he was. Never before had anyone shown her such interest. The gentlemen who visited her childhood home, Moy Castle, always were wary of her brother's presence. The laird's sister was someone to be polite to, but never look at beyond friendship.

Her brother had a way of scaring off most suitors if he thought they were too forward. Her time in London had been tarnished by the nickname she coined. Men stayed away from her for fear of being married off to the women who flocked to her side. She had been glad when she returned home to Moy.

"Perhaps I am. Would it be so bad if I was?"

His eyes twinkled behind his black mask, watching, taking in her every word, her every reaction to him. He was enthralling, made her want things she'd never thought she did before. His lips lifted into a knowing smile, and she had the overwhelming desire to touch her lips to his. To see for herself if his lips were as soft as they appeared.

She inwardly sighed, knowing he would be an excellent kisser. Along with that thought was the disturbing one that other women had enjoyed being in his arms. Women he'd seduced just as he was trying to seduce her. Vixens all.

"It may not be so bad, even if you are English."

He clasped his chest in wounded dramatics. "Do not injure me, Lady Elizabeth. I shall never survive the pain of your rejection."

The strains of a waltz sounded, and she set down her glass of champagne, reaching for Lord Hasting's hand. "Time to dance, my lord. Ye can flatter me on the ballroom floor."

CHAPTER 6

Sebastian smiled, clasped Lady Elizabeth's hand tight as he led her out onto the floor. He pulled her into his arms, holding her close and losing himself in her bright, green eyes. When she wanted to be, she could be quite amusing, more than he thought she would be after their first meeting.

Her hand fit snugly in his, her body perfectly aligned to his height. Dancing with her for the first time made him realize she was quite the perfect height. The idea of seeing her long legs, untying her silk stockings, and sliding them off her satin skin, had him taking a deep, calming breath.

"You mentioned that we're now neighbors, my lord. Have you had Bragdon Manor for long, or is it a recent acquirement?"

"Two years or so. It was the property my brother left me after his death. I should not be the Earl Hastings, you see. I was the second son." Sebastian stopped himself from saying more or revealing that his brother had wanted him to have Bragdon Manor that sat beside Halligale, the estate that Lady Elizabeth now owned.

"Yer brother sounds like a good man to give ye such an impressive estate. I've always admired Bragdon Manor. I would like to see it one day if ye would not mind a visitor."

"I would not mind at all." He pulled her into a quick spin, laughing when she chuckled at his antics. "Tell me, Lady Elizabeth. You say that your brother gave you Halligale. Was the estate always in your family?" he queried, trying to find out how much she knew of the acquirement of the estate.

She shook her head, staring over his shoulder in thought before her eyes met his. "No, it is a new property my brother purchased two years or so ago, I believe. I do adore it, however. Two centuries ago, it was my great-great-grandmother's home on my mother's side. It is nice to have it back in the family."

"Really?" Sebastian said, having not known that tidbit of information. So both he and Elizabeth had an emotional connection to the estate. It made what he was trying to do, ensure a marriage between them, somewhat less brutal, considering he did not love the woman in his arms. That they both loved the estate tempered his guilt to a point. The house should be both of theirs, a home they both should be able to enjoy, not just Elizabeth.

"Did your brother purchase the estate?"

She bit her lip, and he had the distinct impression she was trying to think of something to say other than the truth. "He acquired it when in London, I believe. I do not know the particulars." She met his gaze, studying him a moment. "You're much interested in Halligale, my lord. Why?" she asked bluntly, taking him off guard.

He shook his head, looking beyond her shoulder to watch the dancers about them. "I'm merely curious about my neighbors, that is all." He did not say anything further for fear of saying something that may cause her to suspect him. To win her affections, he needed to be everything she wanted in a husband—caring, flirtatious, enamored. If she found out his sole reason for marrying her was to gain back his childhood home, she would run for the Highlands, and he'd never see her again.

"Perhaps when I visit Bragdon Manor, you may come and see me at Halligale, and your curiosity regarding the estate will be sated." Her fingers slid closer to his nape, and heat licked his skin. The music wound around them, and he took his eyes off the other dancers, turning his attention back to her. She would be a sweet bride to win, and it would be no trouble having her in his bed. He'd enjoy her beneath him, on top of him, before him...

Sebastian swallowed. "You're staring at me, Lady Elizabeth. Do I offend you in some way?" he asked, needing to rein in his wayward thoughts.

"I'm just curious, that is all. Yer are one of the most talked-about gentlemen in Scotland this year. So many are pleased ye have joined our small set of society and are partaking in the Season here. I merely wish to know what would bring an earl, an eligible peer many young debutantes would like to dance with, all the way to Scotland. It is out of the ordinary, I must say."

"Do not tell me that you want me to leave, my lady. Are you so sick of me already?" He was teasing her, but the questions regarding his motivations were strictly off-limits. She did not need to know anything, and if he was careful, she never would.

"I do not know you well enough to know if I wish for you to leave or not, but it is nice having more than our usual set in town."

"It is pleasant being here," he returned, spinning her to a stop as the waltz came to an end. He walked her back to where Lady Julia stood speaking with Lady Georgina. Sebastian bent over Lady Elizabeth's hand, kissing it. "I look forward to dancing with you again soon," he said, turning to search out Rawden.

As much as he would like, he could not spend the entire night with Lady Elizabeth in his arms. He would play the appropriate gentleman and dance with others, but he would seek her out in the later hours. To win one's heart, one must be determined, or so he'd heard matrons of the *ton* tell their charges the few times he'd bothered listening in on their conversations.

He spied Rawden drinking whisky near the terrace doors. Joining him, he procured his own glass of wine from a passing footman. "The ball is going well. How is your chasing of Lady Julia going? You seem quite enamored of her."

Rawden grinned, saluting with his drink. "Very well, thank you. I may even steal a kiss later this evening if I can maneuver her into the gardens."

"Hmm, I wish you well with that." The idea did have merit, and he glanced back to where he'd left Lady Elizabeth, thinking of trying a similar move. Would she be a willing participant in a kiss? If he wished to marry her, he ought to find out if there was any sexual awakening on his part when he kissed her. Certainly, each time he touched her, he was loath to set her aside. A marriage by his estimation would work between them.

"You ought to try it yourself, Hastings. From what I hear, Lady Elizabeth is quite the catch in Scotland, no matter her disastrous Season in London. Did you know that her sister-in-law is the sister to Marchioness Graham and sister to Mr. Stephen Grant, who married Lady Clara Quinton, the Duke of Law's only daughter?"

Sebastian frowned, having quite forgotten the connections Lady Elizabeth had to high society in England. All the more reason she and her extended family never found out why he wished to marry her. Not until the deed was done, at least. They would loathe him for all eternity, tricking their Elizabeth into being his wife, but that wouldn't matter to him, not once he owned Halligale again.

"I had forgotten, you're right."

"Are you still going to continue on with your plan? The moment he finds out that you are courting his sister, her brother is sure to put a stop to it. He will see straight through your interest for what it is. A means of getting back the property he won from your brother at cards. I would suggest, as your friend," Rawden said, crossing his heart with his hand, "to give up the chase. For as much as she's beautiful, witty, and eligible, you will only cause her pain if you trick her into marriage."

Sebastian frowned, turning to Rawden. "Whose side are you on? Are you not supposed to be my friend? Have my back?"

Rawden glared back in turn. "I am your friend, and that is why I caution you on this. If you stop, no one will be hurt, and no Scottish lairds will be out for English blood."

He shrugged. "I like a good sword fight every now and then, and Mackintosh's underhanded ways of winning Halligale from my brother need attending to in any case. I may have to ensure there is no way of her refusing me. I shall have Halligale back then."

Rawden gaped. "You would ruin her to get your way?"

"Others have done it before me." Sebastian looked back to where Elizabeth stood, smiling with her friends, her lips a deep, rosy red that made his blood pump fast in his veins. No, he could not ruin her to get his own way, no matter how much easier that path would be. He wanted her to choose him because she wanted him above anyone else. Not because he had seduced her and they were caught.

"Do stop glaring at me, Rawden. I shall not seduce her. Disregard my earlier comment. I was an ass."

Seemingly satisfied, Rawden nodded, changing the subject to the events that awaited them in Edinburgh on their return. "So from all accounts, we're quite the popular gentlemen this year."

"I had heard," Sebastian said, spying Lady Elizabeth and her friend Lady Julia slipping from the ball through the terrace doors. "Come, we'll gain some fresh Scottish air. The night is surprisingly warm, and it will revitalize us for the late night we're to have."

Rawden agreed, and they walked from the room, stepping out onto the large, stone terrace that overlooked the grounds. There were just as many people out on the terrace as there seemed to be indoors. It made it almost impossible to spy where his quarry had disappeared to.

"She came outside, did she not?" Rawden asked, his tone bored.

"Yes." Sebastian chuckled, pushing ahead. "Come, she left with Lady Julia. Mayhap you can persuade her to dance with you and give me additional time with Lady Elizabeth."

Rawden sighed. "If we must. Lead on."

CHAPTER 7

It took Sebastian several minutes to find Lady Elizabeth and Lady Julia, but eventually he spotted them out on the manicured lawn. Lit lanterns hung from tree to tree, lighting the space. She was talking to a tall Scotsman, and when she reached up, kissing the man's cheeks, a spike of jealous rage tore through him.

Who was this bastard who dared touch her? The man hugged her back, smiling broadly.

Shit, she has a beau?

She turned and spotted him, and her smile widened. "Lord Hastings. Lord Bridgman." She gestured for them to join them. He did so, ignoring the fact his face would not mold into a smile. It seemed stuck at a glower.

"This is an old family friend, Angus, Laird Campbell. He is my brother's best friend since childhood." The fellow clasped Elizabeth's hand, placing it on his arm. He nodded to Sebastian.

"'Tis a pleasure to meet ye, Lord Hastings. I hope ye have been having a lovely time in Scotland."

Sebastian studied them both, wondering if there was

something between them that he was not aware of. Had the man traveled here to be near Elizabeth? To spend time with her away from the madness that was Edinburgh's Season? Did their friendship go beyond platonic?

"We are, thank you. It has been most enjoyable."

The man smiled between them, and for an awkward moment, Sebastian wasn't sure what to say. How to bridge the silence.

Elizabeth gestured to him. "Lord Hastings is going to be my neighbor, Angus. Since meeting his lordship, I have found out that he owns Bragdon Manor beside Halligale. We shall see him often, I think."

"Oh, 'tis a fine estate that one," Laird Campbell said. "When Elizabeth's brother, Laird Mackintosh, came into the estate next to the one ye own, we viewed the property from the boundary. But I imagine ye have others in England?"

"I do, yes, two in fact. Wellsworth Abbey near Netherfield, Nottinghamshire, and a townhouse in London on Grosvenor Square." Not that he would see either of those estates for several months, not if he wished to win the woman currently holding and smiling up at Laird Campbell with something akin to adoration.

Sebastian disliked seeing her so attached to another, and he couldn't fully explain as to why. He knew he wanted her to be his wife. He had to gain back his childhood home, the house where his mother had been born and raised, where he had spent so much time as a boy with his brother before life, and vice, changed him forever. And not for the better.

But why was he feeling so uncomfortable, so annoyed at her holding the laird's arm? He wasn't the jealous type. Seeing a woman he thought to court, or one he may have been seeking out had never before raised such ire, such annoyance in him.

Sebastian swallowed, running a hand through his hair. He

looked back to her and found her watching him, a curious light in her eyes.

"Lady Julia, will you dance with me?" he absently heard Rawden ask, having forgotten his friend altogether. She agreed and left the three of them alone.

Just as he was about to leave, Laird Campbell waved and hollered to a gentleman behind Sebastian. "I do apologize, but I will leave ye now. I will meet you indoors, Elizabeth, and we shall have our dance."

Sebastian nodded his farewell as the man brushed past him, leaving them alone. At last, he had Elizabeth to himself.

"You are fond of the Laird Campbell. I hope I am not keeping you from him."

She raised her chin. The action accentuated her lush lips, still glistening with rouge. "Not at all, my lord. I have known Angus since I was a child. He's more like a brother to me than anything else."

Relief poured through him. She was not lost to him, not yet at least. Not unless she refused his suit and his offer of marriage that he would bestow on her when the time was right. "The gardens are most beautiful this evening. Would you care to stroll about them?"

"If you like," she said, moving off.

Sebastian followed, quickly coming up to amble beside her. "What a shame we're for home tomorrow. I would have liked to have seen more of this grand estate. I do not think I've seen anything more beautiful in all my travels to Scotland."

Lady Elizabeth glanced at the home, towering behind them. "It is picturesque and distinctive. Georgina, Lady Dalton, inherited it after the death of her husband. She loves it, of course, but ye have not seen anything so beautiful until ye have seen my brother's estate and my childhood home, Moy Castle."

"Is the house as grand?" he asked, wanting to keep her talking with him for as long as he could.

"'Tis a castle, with turrets and numerous halls, a great hall that we still use frequently today and a loch of course. No Scottish estate is complete without a loch."

He chuckled. "I couldn't agree more. I hope to see it one day."

She met his eyes and held his attention. For the life of him, Sebastian could not look away. Somehow in the time they had been strolling, they had walked down an abandoned garden path, placing them out of view of the house and terrace.

Music drifted through the trees, and even though no lanterns hung here, he could still make out Elizabeth's pretty face from the moonlight above. She stopped, turning to face him before she reached up and pulled off her mask.

"Ah, that is better. 'Tis so hot under these things."

He ripped his own mask off, glad to be free of it. "I prefer to see you just as you are in any case." He took a step closer to her. "Do you know how stunning you are, Lady Elizabeth?"

She raised one brow, and he could see she was skeptical of his words.

"You do not believe me?"

One shoulder lifted in a delicate shrug. "I have not been the most sought-after lady in either England or Scotland. Do ye not see why I would be wary of such flattery?"

"Because of the name you were called in town. Lucky Lizzie, wasn't it?"

She flinched at the reminder. "It is partly because of that, but also that I have not known ye for long and ye may flatter every woman ye meet in such a way. I am no one special."

He reached out, unable not to feel her. Sebastian ran his finger across her jaw, tipping up her face to look at him. "You are wrong. So wrong. I think you're lovely." He did not know where the words were coming from. All he did know was that they were true. She was unlike any of the simpering fools who followed his coattails in London, hoping for a match. That she was cautious of him, not swayed by his pretty words, meant more to him than he thought they would.

She was different, and he was different when around her. The realization was humbling and telling simultaneously, and he needed to mull on that before their paths crossed again.

A shiver of awareness trembled down her spine at the feel of his touch. They were alone in the gardens, free from prying eyes, and his words, oh, such sweet words, were doing odd things to her stomach.

If she were as bold as Georgina, she would close the space between them and kiss Lord Hastings. The wicked glint in his eyes told her he would not be in opposition to such actions. "Ye think I'm lovely? I think ye may have had too much wine this evening." She grinned, trying to make light of a situation she wasn't entirely sure she had control of. Never had she been in such a position, never had any gentleman touched her so intimately.

It left her discombobulated and unsure of what to do next.

"I have had hardly any wine, my lady. It is not the wine that has intoxicated me."

Oh my. Had he really said such a thing?

"You are not fond of compliments, I think. Mayhap you have not heard enough of them." He reached for her, taking her face in his hands.

Elizabeth gasped, unsure what to do, what to say, or think. Was he going to kiss her? She'd never been kissed before, and now, in his arms, she could not think of anything she wanted more. He was so overwhelming, handsome, his dark-blue eyes and strong jaw, his lips that made her want to close the space between them and touch her mouth to his.

If only she could be so bold.

Like a dream, he slowly leaned down, and then his lips brushed hers. They were as soft as she imagined, and then the kiss changed. He closed his mouth over hers, his tongue slipping against her lips, and a heady ache settled between her legs.

Elizabeth reached for him, wrapping her arms about his neck and slipping into his arms. He let go of her face, wrapping his arms about her waist, crushing her to him. Her breasts grazed against his waistcoat, sensitized and heavier than they normally were.

His mouth moved, teased her to open for him. Elizabeth copied his movements, hoping she was doing the right thing and not making a fool of herself.

"That's it, open for me, darling." He kissed her hard, and then the world on which she stood tilted, threatened to tip her off.

His tongue slid into her mouth, tangling with hers. She moaned, kissing him back with as much need, as much desire as that which coursed through her blood like an elixir.

The kiss went on and on, both of them taking from the other. His hands slid over her back, sometimes lower than what was acceptable in a dance. She wanted him to dip his hand lower still, knead her flesh. On second thought, she wanted his hand elsewhere too. Her breasts ached, her nipples tingled. Liquid heat pooled at her core, and she tightened her thighs, wanting to sate the throbbing there.

Elizabeth fisted his hair into her hands, holding his nape, and slipped her tongue against his. The sensation was odd but delicious. He moaned, and if there ever was a sound she wanted to hear, again and again, it was that one.

She pulled back, meeting his dark, hooded gaze. "Do you like my kiss, my lord?" she said, sipping from his lips yet again.

He swallowed, a small smile quirking his mouth. "I think you need to kiss me again." He closed the space to do exactly that, and Elizabeth stepped away, holding him back with her hand.

"If I kiss ye again now, ye may have your fill, and I cannot have that." She grinned as understanding dawned on his face. He smiled, bowing.

"Good evening, then, Lady Elizabeth."

"Good evening, my lord." Elizabeth turned, biting her lip to stop the squeal of delight from passing through. How delicious it was to be in his arms, to have his kisses bestowed on her. However was she to ensure she received more of them? No man would kiss a woman like Lord Hastings kissed her unless their interest was piqued. Hope blossomed through her. Did this mean that finally she would receive an offer, be courted, flirted with, and kissed for her Season in Scotland?

She smiled, crossing the lawn and stepping back up onto the terrace before heading indoors. Perhaps this year she would be her own good-luck charm and not anyone else's.

Lucky Lizzie indeed.

CHAPTER 8

*T*hey returned to Edinburgh two days later to commence their Season in town. Elizabeth greeted the butler at Georgina's townhouse, handing a nearby footman her gloves and hat. They were all tired after their journey and hectic few days in the country, but Elizabeth couldn't help but feel energized and excited over the weeks to come.

She had watched Lord Hastings leave the country estate the day after the masked ball. Only hours after their kiss in the gardens. He had looked back at the estate before climbing up into the equipage, and she could not help but wonder, hope, that he had been looking for her. Glancing back to see if she were watching him go.

Of course she was watching. She had not stopped thinking of him since the moment he kissed her. Oh, and what a glorious kiss it had been.

He would already be back in Edinburgh, and she hoped he would be at the ball they were attending in a few short hours. Elizabeth strode into the front parlor, going over to the silver salver to see what other events they had been invited to since leaving town.

She shuffled through them all, absently listening to Georgina and Julia discuss their wrinkled traveling gowns before Georgina ordered tea and refreshments in the front drawing room.

"Oh, I'm so happy to be back in town, but what a wonderful masked ball ye threw, Georgina. I'm sure everyone is talking about it," Julia said, slumping down on a nearby chair.

"Of course they are, but I just received word," Elizabeth said, holding up a missive and waving it about, "that Marianne Roxdale is holding an outdoor ball. She states here in her letter that it's to be a reproduction of a night at Covent Gardens in London."

Georgina huffed out an annoyed breath. "She does this to make her event the event of the Season. How dare she compete in such a way and so soon after my own entertainment? It's because I secured Lord Dalton's affections, and she did not. Not that it helped me much since he died two years into our marriage. She's fortunate enough that her husband is still alive."

Julia chuckled, patting the seat beside her for Georgina to sit. "That is quite a callous statement, my dear. It would be best that ye did not state those words again to anyone but us. They will think ye are unfeeling."

"I am unfeeling," Georgiana stated matter-of-fact.

Elizabeth joined them just as their refreshments and sandwiches were brought in. "Do ye think you'll see Lord Bridgman at the ball tonight, Julia? I think he compliments ye well and he seems quite taken with ye, which shows an intelligence otherwise masked by his roguish ways."

Julia grinned. "I may see him tonight, but what I would like an answer to is where you disappeared to on the night of the mask. I saw ye walk off the terrace with Lord Hastings and disappear into the gardens."

Elizabeth had not told her friends what had happened between them. For some reason, she had wanted to keep it to herself, just for her to savor and dream over. During the carriage ride back to Edinburgh, she had ensured they spoke of anything and everything that had nothing to do with the gentleman occupying her life at present.

If she told her friends of her hopes, it would make it doubly worse when he left for London after the Season, and she was still without an offer. The humiliation would be enough if it were simply she who knew her hopes, nevertheless her friends.

"We walked in the gardens, took the air, that is all. Nothing happened between us, and nothing will, I'm sure. We're friends, no more than that."

"Oh," Julia said, disappointment marring her face. "Well, never mind. I'm sure now that we're back in town, and ye have managed to know one another better that he will soon be falling at your silk-slippered feet, begging you to be his wife. No one with any intelligence could deny you."

"I concur. Julia is right. He would be a simpleton if he was not interested in your sweetness."

"We shall see what happens, but I will not get my hopes up, not with Lord Hastings or anyone. I'm in Edinburgh to enjoy the Season here with my two closest friends. That is pleasure enough."

Georgina grinned, sipping her tea. "I agree. Men complicate the situation in any case. They make your mind all fuddled and unable to think straight. When I was married to Lord Dalton, and after our wedding night, I dinna think that I would ever think clearly again. A look, a touch, and I was powerless to his charms." She sighed, throwing them a sad smile. "Until ye have a man who will love ye as Lord Dalton loved me, we shall all keep our options open and not be fooled by pretty words or devastating kisses."

Elizabeth met Georgina's pointed stare and hoped the heat blossoming on her face wasn't visible. Did Georgina know she had kissed Lord Hastings? In the future, she would have to ensure she was more careful. The last thing she needed was to be forced into a marriage with a man who saw her as a diversion during a Season and nothing more. A loveless marriage was a state she could not abide.

Her brother had married for love, adored his wife, and Elizabeth wanted the same sort of commitment. Anything less was not to be borne.

They arrived at the ball later that evening when the event was already in full swing. Each of them, exhausted after their travels, had rested over the afternoon and slept late. Now, refreshed and ready to throw themselves into the full swing of the Season, they entered the room, paying their regards to their hosts before procuring a glass of champagne each from a passing footman.

Marianne Roxdale strolled past, giving them each, but Georgina especially, a cool nod of welcome before disappearing into the crowd.

"I think ye may be right, Georgina dear. Marianne is hosting her outdoor event to spite you. Seems she has not forgiven ye for winning Lord Dalton."

"No, it would most certainly seem that way."

Elizabeth glanced about the room, taking in those who were present. She looked down at her dark-emerald silk gown, the pretty gold embroidery over the bodice a favorite feature of her dress. The color suited her, and she could not help but hope that Lord Hastings was present to see.

A voice in her head taunted her that she'd dressed in one

of her best gowns in the hopes he would see her, be pleased and appreciative of her appearance.

She picked up the diamond-encrusted cross that sat about her neck, fiddling with it, a nervous flutter in her stomach when she could not locate him. There were many parties and balls in the city tonight. He may have attended another event.

"Shall we take a turn about the room?" Georgina said, setting off, Julia by her side.

Elizabeth followed them, stopping to talk to the guests whom she knew. The outdoor ball Marianne Roxdale was holding the *on dit* for conversation.

Leaving the small group a little while later, she turned to find Georgina and Julia but could not see them anywhere. Continuing on, she watched the dancers as she made her way around the room before she ran nose-first into a muscular chest positioned right in front of her.

"Oh, I do beg your pardon," she said, stepping back and holding her glass of champagne out to the side to stop assaulting the gentleman with her drink, along with herself.

"Good evening, Lady Elizabeth."

Shock rippled through her at the silvery words. Her eyes flew up, meeting those of Lord Hastings. "Ye came," she blurted, forgetting herself a moment and wishing she could pull those words back into her mouth. "I mean, good evening, my lord. I did not think ye were here."

"I just arrived," he stated, taking her hand and kissing her gloved fingers. The breath in her lungs seized, and if she were the fainting type, she was sure she would need smelling salts right at this moment. His devilishly handsome face, his eyes that held wicked intent, made her want to forget the ball and just walk out of the room, away from everyone here so they may be alone.

What else could he do to you if you were alone?

The thought came out of nowhere, and heat bloomed on

her face, not the best appearance for a red-headed woman with freckles.

"Will you dance with me?" he asked, not letting go of her hand.

Elizabeth felt herself nod and allowed him to lead her out onto the floor. The strains of a country dance sounded, and couples hurried onto the floor to take their places. Elizabeth stood beside Lord Hastings, feeling as though her heart would burst outside her chest, it pumped so fast. The man made her nervous, made her all jittery inside. Did this mean she liked him as much as she hoped he wanted her? She sent up a silent prayer it was the case and that she would not yet again be labeled Lucky Lizzie for others here in Scotland as well.

The dance started, the steps taking them from each other only to join up yet again. His stormy-blue eyes bored into her, not shifting to the other couples about them. He was all-consuming, made it impossible to concentrate on anything else.

"I'm glad to see you back in town, Lady Elizabeth. I missed saying goodbye to you at Lady Dalton's estate."

"Ye left early, my lord. I was not out of bed by the time you departed," she lied, having been up for several hours, unable to sleep with what happened between them at the ball. The kiss, the clutching, his moan.

Oh dear lord, that sound he had made when she touched her tongue to his. Even now, it made her want to repeat the embrace, hear it again, fell him against her, in her. This must be what her sister-in-law Sophie meant by desiring one's husband, an essential ingredient Sophie had said was required for a happy and enjoyable marriage.

Desire...

Did that mean she desired Lord Hastings? Was this what she was feeling? She also liked him very much, he was amusing and a lovely dancer, but other than that she did not know him much. Only that his brother had passed, and he inherited his father's title.

"I must ask, my lord. What do you like to do when you're not paying court to ladies such as myself or dancing away your nights at balls and parties?"

"Well," he said, twirling her before setting her back in line with the other women dancers. "I take care of my estate. I have not had it for long, you see, and there is much to learn. I'm in Scotland to look over Bragdon Manor as you know, ensure all is in working order before I return to England."

The idea of him leaving for England after the Season shot a pang of sadness through her. If he did not ask her to be his wife and came to know him even better than she did now, she was sure to miss him. Mourn the idea of them she had started to imagine quite more than she should.

"My brother has said I may move to Halligale after the Season, especially if I do not marry. I'm not a young debutante, and my brother does not believe I need to live quite so strictly as an impressionable young woman ought. I shall have my independence, at least, if not a husband."

"Your brother is very accommodating to allow you such freedom. I do not think I would allow my sister—were I to have one—such liberties. Who knows what rogues are lurking about, just waiting for their moment to swoop in and seduce them to scandal?" He waggled his brows, grinning.

Elizabeth laughed. "What fun to be had if they did," she said, teasing him.

"Hmm," he murmured, the sound making her insides quiver. "With me as your neighbor, mayhap, it will be me who'll knock on your door late at night and ask to share a nightcap."

She gasped, and he pulled her against him, spinning her yet again in the dance. "When can we be alone, Lady Elizabeth? I cannot wait much longer to have you in my arms once more." His words whispered against her ear sent delicious shivers down her spine. Did he mean what she thought he did?

"There is no place here for such rendezvous, my lord. You will have to be content to have me in your arms, such as we are now." Although the idea of sneaking away, of allowing him to kiss her as he had before, was more tempting than anything else in the world right now.

He was dangerous, not only to her reputation but to her ability to deny him. She bit back the smile that wanted to burst from her lips. How she loved every moment of his inappropriate words.

And the dark, hungry look he had that promised everything she'd ever wanted and more.

CHAPTER 9

*S*ebastian wasn't sure where the need to have Elizabeth all to himself was coming from, but it was there, as certain as the air he breathed, the wine he drank, he wanted her. The last day of not seeing her had been the longest in his life. It was totally unlike him to constantly think of one particular woman. And yet, that is exactly what he'd one.

He'd wanted to see her on the morning that he'd left Lady Dalton's estate but had not marked her in the breakfast room or any of the other downstairs parlors open to the guests. He wasn't sure what he was going to say to her had she been there. Maybe he needed to remind himself that what they had shared was not an imagined fantasy, that she had kissed him back, sunk into his arms, and allowed him to take his fill of her as much as he'd desired.

He wanted to kiss her again. To feel her pliant and needy in his arms. But how to get her to be alone with him? That was the question.

"Will you come for a drive with me tomorrow? We can travel past Edinburgh Castle or go out into the country if you prefer?" He waited with bated breath to hear her answer, hoping she would say yes.

Her eyes brightened. "I would like that very much."

"Wonderful." He smiled, holding her hand through the dance. He could not remember the last time he looked forward to such an outing. He'd never before invited any particular woman for a carriage drive or to spend the day together. He supposed she would need to bring a maid, but he wasn't so worried about that. Servants knew when to blend into their surroundings and give privacy.

Sebastian reminded himself he was going to all this trouble because he wanted his ancestral home back. Not because he found her enchanting, pretty as a peach and a woman who excited him, made him feel more alive than he had in, well, forever.

"I shall pick you up at eleven if that is agreeable?"

"That will do very well," she replied, smiling up at him as if he'd just bestowed on her a bunch of flowers.

She would suit holding a dozen red roses. It would bring out the fierceness of her hair, make her eyes shine. He leaned close, spinning her and moving her off the ballroom floor and behind a large gathering of potted ferns.

Without warning, he spun her, so she was partially hidden behind him and the plants, and then he did what he'd wanted to do all evening. He kissed her. For a moment, she stilled in his arms, but then like a flower, she opened, bloomed, and kissed him back.

Her fingers slipped around and gripped his lapels, holding him close. By God, his body roared with possession, with need. He took her lips in a punishing kiss, stepping her back farther, if only to prolong his time with her. A bark of laughter pulled him back from the brink of ruining the woman in his arms. He clasped her hand wrapped about his clothing, pulling it away. He breathed deep, putting space between them.

His breathing ragged, Sebastian watched as she too fought to control her reaction to him. Her lips were red, swollen from his touch. Her breasts rose and fell with her heightened breaths, and his body hardened. He damned the ball going on behind them that it stopped him from taking his fill. From kissing her until they were both sated, which, right at this moment, he was decidedly not.

"You should go back to your friends before you are seen behind here with me, Lady Elizabeth."

Her eyes widened farther, and then she was gone, brushing past him, the scent of lavender all that remained. Sebastian closed his eyes, breathing deep and calming his racing heart. For how long he stood there, gaining control of his emotions, of his needs, he could not say, but tomorrow, *tomorrow*, he would see her again. Alone this time, save her servant and for as long as they both wished.

Edinburgh had fewer eyes than London, and he was starting to enjoy his time here more than he thought he would. Winning the heart of a Scottish lass was turning out to be more enjoyable than first thought. Now he just needed to ensure he did not lose it just as his brother lost their estate.

*E*lizabeth paced in the front foyer of Georgina's Edinburgh home, listening for a carriage to roll to a stop out the front of the house. She stopped every now and then and peeked out the front windows beside the door, careful not to move the lace curtains that hung there, lest Lord Hastings made an appearance and she was seen as too eager.

And she was impatient to be gone, alone with his lordship. Her maid sat on a nearby chair, a book clasped tight in her hands and not the least interested in what Elizabeth was doing. After their kiss last night, she'd barely slept. The thought that he'd snuck her behind some palms and kissed her until her toes curled in her silk slippers shocked her still. Her heart beat fast at the memory of it and her stomach clenched in delicious flutters.

Would he kiss her again today? Something told her he would, that the sole reason for inviting her out on this ride was to be alone with her, just the two of them. Her maid could be distracted easily enough and not be bothered too much by what Elizabeth did. Not that she intended to ruin herself, but a kiss could not hurt, surely.

A highly sprung black, open carriage rolled to a stop, and she knew he was here. His lordship tied the reins to the carriage before jumping down with carefree ability she wished she could enjoy. Having to wear a dress most of the time stopped her from having such freedoms. But none of that mattered, not right now.

She stood at the window, admiring the sight of him walking up the steps to the front door, his dark hair falling over one eye and giving a roguish edge to his appearance.

There was a small smile playing about his mouth, and she hoped he was as eager for their outing as she was. This was her first such foray with a gentleman, and she couldn't help but hope that it was true. That he was genuine in his regard of her and wasn't playing her a fool.

It would be a great lark indeed to deceive Lucky Lizzie in her home country as well as England.

A rap on the door sounded, and she stood aside, allowed the footman to open the door. Elizabeth met Lord Hastings as he stepped onto the foyer's parquetry floor, giving him her hand. "Lord Hastings. You are most prompt," she said, not letting him know that she was as well. That for the past half hour, she had been in this foyer waiting for him.

"I never leave a beautiful woman waiting." He reached for her hand, kissing it, his eyes meeting hers as his lips touched her glove. Heat thrummed through her, and she took a calming breath. Her reactions to him were maddening and sweet, all at the same time. She loved what he did to her, but it frightened her too. There was so much at stake, her heart for one, should he be the type of gentleman who paid court during his time in town only to turn about and leave without a backward glance or offer.

The humiliation, the hurt, would be unbearable.

She fought not to grin like a debutante on her first turn about the dance floor. He held out his arm, and she allowed him to help her down the steps toward his carriage. The day was warm, not a cloud in the sky, a perfect day to visit and explore Edinburgh and its surrounding lands.

Her maid perched herself on the back of the equipage, and they were soon rumbling up the hill toward the ancient fortress. They could not get too close, only the Royal Mile, due to the castle being an army garrison. Lord Hastings pulled the horses to a stop, and for a moment, they stared up at the high walls, the shouts of men behind the building's walls barely audible.

His lordship turned the equipage about, heading back along the mile toward Holyrood House. The palace gates were too closed, yet the sight of the beautiful gardens beyond all but begged to be explored. "I wonder if the royal family is in residence." she said, staring at the magnificent building.

"I do not believe so," he replied, clicking his tongue to move the horses on. "We shall drive to Arthur's Seat. I assume you know where I'm taking you."

"Of course." Elizabeth adjusted the small blanket that sat over her legs, already enjoying herself immensely, even though they had not traveled far or seen too much. "We used to picnic there as children when we came to Edinburgh with Mama. I will admit that my seeing it again is long overdue," she said.

"Well then, I'm glad to be the one to reacquaint you."

His sweet smile made warmth flow through her veins. This courting business was really quite lovely, especially when one enjoyed being courted and found the man quite to her tastes.

No man would go to all this trouble to merely turn about at the end of the Season and leave. Oh no, it was looking almost certain Lord Hastings was leading up to ask her to be his bride.

Would she say yes if he did? She shot a look at him, inwardly sighing at the sight of his perfect profile. His lovely, dark hair was long enough for the breeze to flutter as they trotted through the streets of Edinburgh.

Yes, she would agree to marry him should he ask, and she would revel in every kiss and touch he bestowed on her from that moment on.

Her heart beat fast, as she imagined being his wife. If she were fortunate enough to have a marriage with affection and love like her brother and Sophie enjoyed, she would be well pleased. Could this be where they were headed? He certainly seemed to like her.

No more Lucky Lizzie for others, but for herself.

They made the base of Arthur's Seat on Edinburgh's outskirts just as the sun rose high in the sky. Lord Hastings jumped down, coming around to help her alight. She reached for him, placing her hands on his shoulders. A squeal rent the air when he pulled her from the carriage, lifting her as if she weighed nothing but a feather. His action slipped her against him, and, with devastating slowness, he dropped her to her feet.

Elizabeth felt every muscle in his chest, every flex of his arms, the warmth of his breath against her face, his closeness that made her forget herself, before her toes hit the ground.

Absently she heard her maid jump down, but she couldn't foster enough caution to step away and out of his hold. His gaze held hers, a promise of some kind lighting his eyes.

"This way," he said, taking her hand and starting up a well-worn path lined with the undergrowth from the trees.

"Have you ever been here before?" she asked him as they came to a clearing. Lord Hastings let go of her hand at the sight of other people and placed it on his arm instead.

"Once, several years ago now, but it has not changed. I should have thought to bring a picnic basket and blanket so that we could have shared and enjoyed a meal."

"Perhaps next time," she suggested, hoping there would be more of these carefree days, away from Society's eagle eye.

"I would like that," he said, cocking his head to one side. "Come, we shall walk a little farther."

"Tell me, Lord Hastings, do you visit Scotland often now that you have an estate here?" She hoped he would, that he would make Scotland his permanent home, especially if he offered for her hand. She could quite happily live in her home country with the man she was starting to care about above anyone else in the world.

"I do, at least once a year, for several months. My English estate in Nottinghamshire, while beautiful, is not where my heart resides. My childhood was spent more in Scotland than in England, and I have always said it is more my home here than anywhere else."

"Really?" Elizabeth met his gaze. "But I thought your home in Scotland was recently acquired. Did you used to live elsewhere, or did your family have a home that you have not told me?"

CHAPTER 10

Sebastian stilled, his mind whirling to form a reply and to remember all the lies he'd told so far. Lady Elizabeth was no fool, and one slip of the tongue from him and his ability to win her, win back his estate, would be over.

He wished he could swallow his own stupid tongue. How to get out of this mess of words he'd created? "My mother was Scottish and had a home here, but I was too small to remember where." He closed his eyes a moment, hating the fact he'd just made himself sound like an idiot.

"How lovely that ye have a connection here too. I like ye even more now."

Her teasing words made his blood burn. Damn the maid who followed them a few steps back. He wanted Elizabeth alone so he could kiss that delectable, pouty mouth. Somehow in the few days that he knew her, she had started to wiggle her way under his skin, and he had at times had to remind himself the reason he was courting her in the first place.

To gain back Halligale. Become the lord of the grand Scottish estate that Lady Elizabeth's brother stole in a baseless game of cards. Not because she made him want to be around her, made him look forward to each new day he woke up for on this great land.

"When do you think you shall return to Halligale?" he asked, needing to change the subject off of himself.

"At the end of the Season. My brother has said that I can live there so long as I have a companion or husband." She threw him a curious look. "Ye too must be for Bragdon Manor soon. I will not forget that ye promised me a tour."

The idea of having Elizabeth alone with him at his home made him almost groan aloud. What fun they could have if that were the case. "I have not forgotten. I should like to have you in my home for more than a visit if you were open to the idea."

She stopped walking, staring up at him. A small frown marred her brow. "I apologize, Lord Hastings, but can you ask that question again to ensure I heard you correctly, for I'm not entirely certain of your meaning."

Sebastian glanced at the maid. "Please turn about a moment and ignore all that you're about to hear," he said to the young woman.

"Yes, my lord." The young woman turned about without questioning his decree.

"Lady Elizabeth Mackintosh, would you be willing to marry me? I know that we have not known each other long, but I do believe we suit." He had not meant to ask her so soon. Hell, he barely knew her, but what was the point in delaying his suit? He liked her and he needed her to gain back his ancestral estate. There was no point in postponing the inevitable. She would either say yes, or he would have to persuade her to do so.

She stared up at him, her eyes wide in shock. "You're asking me to marry you?"

He nodded. "I am." He leaned close, kissing her cheek, the

lobe of her ear, her neck. She shivered in his arms, and he smiled against her neck, breathing deep her sweet lavender scent. "Say yes and marry me so we can be together without a maid in tow."

She gasped, her hand reaching out to lay on his chest. She pushed him back a step and met his gaze, hers cloudy with desire. Heat licked along his spine that she was so attuned to him. That her reaction to him was so alike his own. Made him burn with a longing that cried to be sated. How fortunate that the woman he needed to marry made him react so.

"Ye are not trying to fool me, my lord? Ye are in earnest?" she asked him.

Sebastian had the overwhelming desire to strangle the gentlemen in London, and ladies too, who had teased her. Made her believe she was useful to gain other people offers of marriage and not one for herself. The fact he too was fooling her made his stomach churn. He did not wish to hurt her and telling her the truth of why he wanted the alliance would surely do that.

No, this was better. If she agreed to be his wife, he could marry her, gain Halligale back, and Elizabeth would never be the wiser. What one did not know would not hurt them, as the saying went.

Her brother will work out your motive.

Sebastian pushed the unhelpful thought aside. he'd worry about that when it happened. "I want you, and no one else. I promise you that, above my honor as a gentleman." Which was also true. He did want her, and no one else. The mere idea of her marrying someone else made him want to gnash his teeth. "Marry me, Lady Elizabeth. Be my wife."

She smiled, her pretty mouth tempting him before she said the words that placed him one step closer to his home. "Yes, my lord. I shall marry you."

He whooped, picking her up and spinning her about

before taking her lips in a searing kiss. She kissed him back, held nothing from him, even though they could be come upon at any moment.

"Call me Sebastian. No more my lord or Hastings. To you, I'm merely Sebastian." He kissed the smile off her face, enjoyed her reaction to him, the bank of desire she released in him each time he was with her.

"Ye may call me Elizabeth in return," she said, wrapping her arms about his neck, her smile as warm as the sunshine on his back.

Sebastian liked the pleasure his proposal brought forth in her. To make her happy made him so. It was a novel experience, one he'd not experienced before with a woman. He liked it. He liked her.

"When shall we announce it? I need to write to my brother."

The idea of telling her brother tempered his enjoyment. He was an intelligent man from all reports, and Rawden was right. He would suspect his motives. Undoubtedly know he was the late Lord Hasting's brother and see his proposal for what it was.

"May we postpone telling your brother?" he asked her.

Her shoulders slumped, and he knew he'd disappointed her. Sebastian pulled her into his arms, holding her tight. "I do not say this to upset you or cause you to doubt my offer. I merely want to enjoy the Season here with you a while longer before the madness of a wedding pulls you back to Moy and your family. I do not wish for you to leave."

Her fingers played with his hair. Damn it all to hell, she was sweet and his if he could manage to keep her. Keep her brother from ripping her from his arms.

"I understand, and I shall not tell Brice, but," she said, looking up at him with beseeching eyes that he feared he'd never deny. "May I tell my friends? I would like to share my happy news with them."

Sebastian saw no impediment to that idea. "Of course, I would love them to share in your happiness."

She leaned up, surprising him with a kiss, and he took the opportunity afforded him and kissed her back. The kiss spiraled into something that was hot, needy, and altogether not appropriate for where they stood. They needed to marry and soon. He wasn't sure he could live without her in his bed every night for too much longer.

So long as her brother didn't cause him any more trouble, more than he already had. He would not lose Elizabeth, or his childhood home for a second time.

CHAPTER 11

Elizabeth stared at her friends, hoping the shock of her betrothal would enable them to speak, and soon. Both women stared at her, mouths agape, their eyes wide.

"Say something, will you? Ye know I dinna like it when ye do not state your opinion."

Georgina spoke fist, blinking out of her stupor. "You're marrying Earl Hastings? When did he start courting ye in earnest?"

"More importantly," Julia stated, her mouth still gaping. "How did I miss his interest in ye went beyond innocent flirtation to an offer of marriage!"

Elizabeth held out her hands, calling for calm. "It's been a whirlwind, I know. My brother has not even been informed, but I think Sebastian and I suit. He's amusing, attentive." She wanted to go on and tell her friends his kisses were devastatingly toe-curling, but she did not. Some things she wanted to keep just for them, their own sweet secret. "I like him, and he grew up in Scotland at his mother's estate, so he understands the country and our way of life here."

"He's English. What will ye brother say, do ye think?" Julia asked, sitting back on her chair and crossing her legs up under her.

"Brice married an English woman. I dinna think he'll care."

Georgina laughed, a tinkling sound that held an edge of sarcasm. "Oh, he'll care. While Julia and I both enjoy the company of an Englishman at balls and parties, it is no secret that our family would prefer a Scotsman to be our husbands. Yer brother may have married a Sassenach, but that dinna mean he wants ye to marry an Englishman. Yer brother will be no different."

Elizabeth bit her lip, worrying it between her teeth. Would Brice dislike her choice? She did not like the idea of her brother being against her marriage. She wanted Brice and Sebastian to become friends as well as brothers-in-law. To share their children's childhoods, spend Christmas together, and more Seasons in town both here and in England.

"I dinna believe so. Brice will be happy for me and my choice. He'll not cause any difficulty, I'm sure."

Julia raised her brow. "When do ye think you'll tell your brother?"

Elizabeth frowned, unsure herself when that would happen. "He's preoccupied at home at the moment. Sophie is *enceinte*, and there are complications. I dinna want him rushing to Edinburgh to approve my impending marriage. I would prefer to travel home and let him know in a few weeks." Or, the idea of arriving home already married was tempting as well. Her brother could not disapprove of her Englishman then.

Not that she expected him to dislike Sebastian. English or no, there was nothing wrong with her choice. He was titled, rich, sweet, and kind. What was there to dislike?

"Oh, my dearest, why did ye not tell us about Sophie? We will both hope for the best for her."

Elizabeth smiled at her friends. "Thank ye for your kind thoughts. Her brother and his wife Lady Clara have arrived to assist them, but I'm to return home at the end of the Season before the child is due."

"What does Lord Hastings think of postponing ye telling your brother?" Julia asked, watching her keenly.

The look on her friend's face made her choose her words carefully, not wanting to let them know that it was, in fact, Sebastian's idea not to tell Brice. To give them time to enjoy more of the Season, just the two of them, before the madness of a betrothal sent Edinburgh into a flurry and her family along with it.

"He is happy to comply with my wishes." Elizabeth pasted on a smile, willing the seed of doubt that settled in her stomach that he had not wanted to tell her brother because, by the end of the Season, he intended to cry off and return to England.

No, he wouldn't do that to her. Elizabeth had to move away from the doubt Lucky Lizzie had instilled in her. His courtship, his affections were true.

She swallowed the panic threatening to bring up her breakfast. "I hope you're both happy for me. For all that the situation has come about quickly, I am happy with my choice. I think that given more time I could fall in love with my husband."

Georgiana smiled, standing and pulling her up to give her a tight hug. "We're happy for ye, Elizabeth. Lord Hastings is a lovely man, and if he has captured your heart or is on the way to doing so, how could we not love him in turn?"

Tears sprung to her eyes, and she hugged her friend back, laughing when Julia joined in with their show of affection.

"Ye know what this calls for," Julia said, not letting either of them go. "We need to go shopping for your wedding night. A lovely nightgown is required for these Englishmen with a profile and jaw, such as Lord Hastings has. You need to shock his stockings off when he sees you for the first time alone in a bedchamber."

Butterflies took flight in her stomach at the thought of being alone with Sebastian in such a way. She supposed that would happen soon, and a new wardrobe would be required. As the new wife of an earl, she had to look her best. She had waited years to be married and to be able to wear whatever she wished. Rich, dark colors that suited her red hair and pale skin.

*S*ebastian leaned against the wall at the Season's latest event. A day after proposing to Elizabeth, and he could not keep his gaze from following her about the room as she waltzed with Lord Fairfax. There was something different about her tonight. Her smile was brighter, her eyes more alive, and as for her dress, well, he did not think he'd seen anyone more beautiful in his life.

He reminded himself their marriage, was a means to an end. A way in which he could gain control of his ancestral home his brother lost. To Elizabeth, however, he had started to think that she cared for him more than he deserved.

He didn't like to deceive her. It wasn't her fault his brother had been an ass and lost their estate in a game of cards, but neither should Elizabeth's brother been so quick to take advantage of his stupid sibling.

A quiet voice told him Laird Mackintosh was free of any misconduct just as much as his sister.

He rolled his shoulders, his eyes narrowed when Lord Fairfax's arm slid low on Elizabeth's back, and she was forced to reach around and lift it away from her derrière.

Her gaze met his over the gentleman's shoulder, and she threw him a wink. Sebastian choked on his whisky, receiving a whack across his back from Rawden for his effort.

"Whoa, Hastings. We don't need you to choke to death before you make that delectable Scottish morsel your wife. I'm assuming by your glower that you've laid claim and asked her to be your bride as planned."

He nodded once, clearing his throat. "I have, and she said yes. As for Lord Fairfax, if his hand moves lower again on her person, I will be forced to break his arm before the waltz ends."

Rawden chuckled, a knowing light in his eyes. "Talking of women, I must say Lady Julia is driving me to distraction. Since our return to town, she has refused me each time I've asked her to dance or stroll about a ballroom. I think she is testing me in some way."

"Or she is trying to let you know in the nicest possible way that she is not interested in you."

Rawden looked at him as if he'd sprouted two heads. "Don't be absurd, man. How could she not! I'm the second son of a duke. An alliance with my family would benefit anyone."

"Except she's an heiress with her own estate here in Scotland. She no sooner needs to marry you than Lady Elizabeth needs to marry me. I, however," he said, throwing his friend a smug glance, "just happen to be more fortunate than you in that I have secured my bride's affections."

"She isn't your bride yet," Rawden reminded him, gesturing to the two women as they were reacquainted after Elizabeth's dance. "What are you going to do if her brother refuses your suit?"

Sebastian had been thinking about the issue, which was foremost in his mind. If Elizabeth heard of his brother's gambling problem that led to his ancestral home being lost to a game of cards and that the house in question was now her dowry, she would run for the Highlands and never marry him.

"I'm thinking of eloping with her. Now that she has agreed to be my wife, and she's of age, I do not see the impediment. We could return to Moy Castle, inform her brother of her married state, and deal with the fallout then. I will be sure to consummate the marriage before then."

Sebastian took a deep, calming breath as the idea of having Elizabeth beside him, under him, on top of him sent a lick of heat up his spine. It would be no chore to make the fiery redheaded Scotswoman his. He looked forward to plundering her. In fact, the idea kept him awake most nights since he'd met her.

Rawden whistled. "He'll call you out or just murder you if you marry her without him knowing. From what I know of Laird Mackintosh, he's not a small lad and not one to be crossed."

Sebastian sipped his whisky, thinking over his friend's words. "Married and with the union consummated, there would be nothing he could do. He certainly would not want to kill his sister's husband. And with Halligale back in my hands, should Elizabeth take offense to the truth, at least I have time to win her back, try to make her see my side of the argument. She may be angry for some time, but I believe that too shall pass."

"Do you really think that'll happen? She will never forgive you if she finds out that you're marrying her for her property. If she did not have it in her name, would you be in Scotland right now chasing her skirts about?"

No, Sebastian would not, but that was beside the point. It also didn't factor, not anymore. There was something about Elizabeth that he liked. He enjoyed her company, was glad to have met her, to have her as his wife. They suited, no matter what the reasons were for bringing him here in the first place.

"I will have to try to ensure the truth does not pull us apart."

"You sound like a man falling in love and regretting his choice. I wish you luck with that, Sebastian," Rawden said, stepping out into the fray of guests and disappearing soon after.

He could make Elizabeth understand, explain how much Halligale meant to him. If she knew the truth, she would forgive him eventually. After all, it was not as if he did not like her. He did very much. More than anyone he'd ever met before in his life.

CHAPTER 12

A hand reached up and smoothed the line between his brow, and he realized Elizabeth was standing before him, a precious, knowing smile on her lips.

"You're woolgathering, my lord. Penny for yer thoughts?" she asked him, stepping to stand beside him.

He picked up her hand, kissing it and not caring who noticed. Her eyes widened, and he grinned. "Good evening, my dearest. I see I was too late to claim you for the waltz."

She chuckled, wrapping her arm tight about his and holding him close. "There is to be another. I have been assured of that from our hostess this evening."

It pleased him that she wanted to reassure him. He wished the gnawing ache in his gut would also dissipate. However, something told him that it would not, not until he told her the truth and faced the consequences.

"I'm glad to hear it," he replied, tugging her to walk with him. He needed to move, to remove them from the gathered throng. He needed to have her to himself. "We should leave. I need to speak to you alone."

Her eyes widened, but she nodded. "I can tell Julia and

Georgina I have a headache and need to return home, but we need to be careful to leave separately, so as not to raise suspicion, if you dinna want my brother to know of your suit. Everyone in Edinburgh knows him, and no doubt are updating him weekly on my progress."

Sebastian had not thought of such a thing, which made his need to get her away from Edinburgh, away from her brother's reach, more imperative. "Have your carriage take you home. I shall meet you there."

She nodded, sending him a small, conspiratorial smile, and then she was gone. He watched her disappear into the throng and wondered when he'd become such a cad. A bastard who offered marriage to a lady who was as high on the peerage ladder as he, who was as kind and sweet as anyone he knew, and all for an estate.

Who had he become?

Elizabeth did as Sebastian asked, meeting him at the mews behind Georgina's townhouse. He pulled her up into his carriage just as it rolled to a stop, calling out the address as he slammed the door closed.

"Why are we going to Dalmahoy?" she asked, as the carriage lurched forward. "That is an hour away, at least."

"I need to discuss something with you, and I need you not to answer the question until you at least ponder it a moment in your mind."

"Very well," she conceded, settling back on the leather squabs and clasping her hands in her lap. "I'm listening."

He took a fortifying breath. "I do not wish to wait for your brother or the banns to be called. I want to marry you now. I want you to be mine and no one else's. From this night forward."

For a moment, Elizabeth fought to control her racing

heart. The idea of being his, of him wanting to marry her now and not in several weeks, soothed the small amount of anxiety she had had over his request to wait.

It seemed his lordship had a change of heart. "Why do you wish to marry me now? I haven't even told my brother that you asked me. Do you even have a special license?"

He glanced down at her hands in his, studying them, playing with her fingers. "I do not do this to steal you away from your family, but why wait, Elizabeth? The Season is young, and I do not want to spend it having to keep my hands off you. Being careful how I touch you and what I say. I want you, more than you'll ever know. More than I thought I would ever want anyone."

His words melted her heart, and she sighed. "This is all such a rush, Sebastian." Her stomach churned in knots. "You're not trying to deceive me in any way, are ye?" She had to ask. She would be a fool not to.

He swallowed, reaching for her face. "No, of course not," he managed. "Know this for it is true. I want to marry you because I adore you. I want you to be my wife, my countess. I want you because I desire you so dearly. The thought of anyone touching you, Lord Fairfax in particular after his wandering hands this evening, made me want to throttle the bastard. Never doubt those words for they are true."

Elizabeth met his gaze, trying to settle her nerves over what he was saying, hoping he wasn't playing her the fool. "So we're to Dalmahoy then?" she asked, smiling a little.

"If you say yes to my proposal, my plan, then yes."

She thought about it a moment, but she already knew what her choice would be. "Yes, let us elope, and then I can return home and celebrate with my family. They will be overjoyed to know that I'm married. We can always take our vows again in the chapel at Moy Castle."

He kissed her quickly, meeting her eye before he said, "I would adore that, just as I adore you."

Sebastian pulled her into his arms and kissed her hard. She opened for him immediately, no fear, no hesitation, and his body roared with need. He should be kissing her with sweet, luring strokes, but he could not. His body, his mind had other ideas. Tonight when he'd seen her dancing with Lord Fairfax, he'd all but had to force himself to remain where he was. It would be impossible for him to stand aside, watch her be courted by other men this Season, and all the while be secretly engaged to her.

No. He could not endure it. He wanted to dance, to flirt, and be inappropriate with her if they wished before society. He did not want to watch his manners or his conduct. If he wished to kiss her in the middle of a waltz at a ball, then he damn well would.

She pushed into his arms, her breasts grazing his chest, and his wits spiraled, crumbled into a pile of rubble.

He wanted her with a longing that would take out his knees had he not been seated. His body burned, hardened, and he wanted her to touch him, to run her hands over his body, clasp, and stroke him, give him pleasure.

She moaned, and he realized his hand was kneading her breast, rolling her nipple between his thumb and forefinger. He needed to see it, to taste, and revel in her warmth.

Sebastian broke the kiss, pleased when she lay her head back, pushing her breast into his hand. He ran his finger along the top of her gown. "Your skin is so unblemished, like milk." He slowly slipped her bodice down with patience he did not know he possessed, exposing her flesh. He could not wait a moment longer. He dipped his head and kissed her pebbled peak, licking its pinkened surface, making it bead farther.

Her fingers spiked into his hair, pulling him near. He fought for control. He would not take her here, in a carriage of all places. She was a maid, a lady, and soon to be his wife. She deserved better than this. With a strength he did not know he possessed, he wrenched away, breathing deep to control his need.

Sebastian threw himself into the squabs, facing forward, and refused to look at her mussed hair, her flushed face, and swollen, well-kissed lips as she set her gown to rights.

He looked out the window and found they were not far from the small village where he had organized the reverend at St. Mary's church to marry them.

She reached out, touching his arm, and he closed his eyes, fighting not to wrench her onto his lap and continue what they had started.

"Sebastian, what is the matter?" she asked, trying to catch his eye.

He shook his head, grinding his teeth. "We're not married yet. I should not have touched you as I did."

A seductive, knowing chuckle sounded at his ear, and he shivered. She leaned close, clasping the lapels of his jacket. "You dinna see me stopping ye."

He took a calming breath. "I know, but it does not make it right. I want to marry you, and I do not want to ruin you in this way. You deserve better than a romp in a moving carriage."

She bestowed the loveliest smile, and it was equal to a fist to the stomach. He ought to tell the truth. Tell her that his courting of her had been born out of greed. The need to have his ancestral home back and nothing else.

But how could he tell her such a thing? She would never marry him then, and that goal had now changed. Morphed into something new and real, something true that made his heart full.

"You said you would marry me," he continued. "I have a reverend waiting for us. Married acquaintances of mine who live on an estate just outside of Dalmahoy will meet us at the church and be witnesses to our vows."

"However did you organize all this so soon?" she asked him, her eyes bright with wonder and excitement.

"You are over one and twenty, so we do not need your family's approval. I paid a hefty fee today to secure a special license. Not easily found here in Edinburgh. Our union will be legal, then nothing can come between us."

The carriage lurched to a stop, and Sebastian turned to her, taking her hand. "We're here. Are you ready, Lady Elizabeth to become Countess Hastings?"

She squeezed his hand in return, nodding once. "I am ready."

And so was he.

CHAPTER 13

*E*lizabeth walked up the aisle alone, wishing her family could be here with her, and yet, overjoyed at the idea that she was about to marry a man she adored. Seeing Sebastian waiting for her before a stone altar, the reverend smiling as he stood with his bible in hand, made butterflies take flight in her stomach. Soon she would be his, and she could be with him always. A small part of her had to admit she was marrying him for more than the mere reason she enjoyed his company and found him amusing, not to mention, devastatingly alluring.

Her heart had been speared by love's arrow, and for several days now, she had come to realize she did not merely like Sebastian, but loved him. Loved his humor, his conversation, and kisses. His hot, commanding gaze that even from across a room made her skin singe.

After all the legalities were dealt with, the thought that she would be alone with him, and as his wife, set her senses rioting.

Absently she heard the reverend declare them husband and wife, and before she had a chance to thank the father, she was caught up in Sebastian's arms, his mouth taking hers in a searing kiss.

Elizabeth wrapped her arms around his neck, kissing him back. The day was simply perfect, and when she returned home to Moy, she would celebrate with her family and friends, but tonight, right now, was her time. A time to savor with her new husband.

He set her back down on her silk slippers before turning to his friends and the reverend. "Thank you for tonight. I shall not forget your kindness for our sake."

"You are most welcome, Hastings," Lord Pitt said, smiling at them both and holding his wife's hand atop his arm. "I took the liberty of preparing a room at our estate if you wish to rest."

"That is most kind, Pitt. I do not know how to thank you," Sebastian said, smiling down at Elizabeth a moment.

"Ah, it is no trouble at all," his lordship said, waving Sebastian's concerns aside. "There are plenty of rooms at the big house, no need for thanks."

They quickly signed the register, making their union legal, before Sebastian paid the reverend handsomely and they were on their way. Soon they arrived at the dark-gray stone home of Lord and Lady Pitt, where they would spend their wedding night.

During the short journey neither of them spoke, but Sebastian held her close, his arm about her shoulder, his thumb idly sliding against the skin on her arm and sending her wits to spiral.

She could not wait for them to be alone.

They made their way upstairs. The mansion with its dark, rich woods and heavy window coverings was too sullen for Elizabeth's taste, but it was still opulent and comfortable. Lady Pitt pointed out several rooms, the servant's stairs, the upstairs parlor if they cared to use it. Finally, they came to their room, and she gestured them inside, looking about and checking everything was in order.

"If you need anything, ring for a servant, the bellpull is beside the mantel, and they will assist you." Lady Pitt wished them good night and closed the door softly behind her.

Elizabeth walked about the room, taking in the furnishings of rich, mahogany wood and deep-green velvet coverings both on the bed and the chairs that sat before the fire. Animal skins covered the wooden floors and the curtains had been pulled closed to keep out the night's chill.

She went and stood before the fire, turning to face Sebastian, who leaned against the door, slowly untying his cravat, his wicked, heated gaze focused solely on her.

Heat pooled at her core, and she could hardly wait for him to touch her. To be with him as a wife should be with a husband.

"When you stand before a fire, I can almost see through your gown. Did you know that?"

She flushed but did not move. Instead, she reached up, pulling out the pins in her hair and letting her long, red locks fall about her shoulders. "No, I did not know, but I thank ye for letting me be aware of the fact. I'll be sure not to stand before any fires when I'm next in a ballroom."

"You have lovely legs, wife," he said, stepping closer still, his jacket and waistcoat thrown onto a nearby chair without care. His hands reached down, pulling his shirt out of his buckskin breeches. He reached behind his head, slipping it off.

Elizabeth swallowed, having never seen him naked before. A delicious part of her reveled in the knowledge he was hers to admire, to have. That no one else would ever see him thus again. Not unless that person was her. She met him halfway across the room, not willing to sit idly by, wait for him to take her in his arms.

He pulled her close and shuffled her toward the four-poster bed, making quick work of the hooks at the back of her ballgown. Before she had a chance to be shy, he'd stripped her of her gown and shift, turning her quickly to unlace her corset.

Sebastian stood back and took her in, his eyes running over her body like a physical caress. Elizabeth took a calming breath, unsure of what was going to happen, what was expected of her. If he liked what he saw.

"Dear God, you're stunning." He scooped her into his arms and deposited her in the middle of the bed, following and pinning her beneath him.

She slid her foot along his calf, the feel of his hairy legs tickling the base of her feet. He still wore his breeches, a fact that now with her beneath him, she wanted to amend. "Undress, Sebastian. I want to feel you."

He kissed her quickly before kneeling on the bed. Like his other clothes, he made short work of his breeches, throwing them somewhere on the floor at the base of the bed. Her mouth dried, her eyes fixed on his manhood. She swallowed, nerves pooling in her stomach and something else, a warmth, a need, at the sight of him.

Would they even fit together?

As if reading her thoughts, he chuckled. "We'll fit, my darling." He joined her, kissing her deep and eliminating all the fear that had spiked through her at the sight of his sex.

Their tongues tangled, and heat pooled at her core. She undulated against him, her body afire, and seeking something she did not know but was certain she would soon understand.

He surged against where she burned, and pleasure spiked through her blood. She gasped, clutching at his back as they kissed deep and long, as he prepared to make her his.

It was too much. She needed him now. Enough with the

teasing. They had played that game. Now it was time for her to have him fully. To claim him for herself.

"From the moment I saw you, I wanted you," he admitted, a truth that had nothing to do with why he'd married Elizabeth, but certainly why he pursued her without caution. She was a beautiful woman, but what made her especially different from all the rest in his vicinity was her intellect, her kindness. A woman like her should have been scooped up and married years ago. She should have a hoard of children already.

The thought that tonight he could get her with a child, that she could grow round with his children, fortified his growing feelings for her. Emotions he could no longer deny. He had long ended merely liking her. He now realized, with trepidation, he was falling in love with her.

"Did ye really?" she gasped, arching her back and giving him the ability to kiss her neck, the tops of her breasts. Her skin was flushed, her hair long strands of red hair curled about the pillows. His heart stuttered.

She was so beautiful it hurt.

"What did you think of me?" he questioned her, kneading one breast, bringing it up to his mouth to kiss and tease.

She moaned, trembling beneath him. "I thought you extremely handsome, but English," she teased, watching him as he licked her nipple. Their eyes met, and he teasingly bit her flesh. Elizabeth pouted but purred, spiking her fingers in his hair to hold him against her.

He wasn't going anywhere. Tonight was just for them, and he would savor every minute he had her in his arms. A gentleman partook in one first night with his wife, and Sebastian wanted to make the most of it with Elizabeth.

Her skin smelled of jasmine, and he kissed his way

down her stomach. Her breathing was ragged, and he intended to make it a lot more so before their night was over.

He pushed her legs apart, sliding his hand on the inside of her thigh, running his finger across her mons. She moaned his name, clutching him.

"Do you trust me?" he asked her, settling between her legs.

She nodded, watching him with wide, clear eyes. He kissed between her legs, smiling that it was the same shade as her head before kissing her fully. She gasped, tried to twist out of his hold, but he held her still, suckled on her sensitive nubbin. Within a moment, she stopped, waited to see what he did next. He teased her flesh, kissed and licked his way along her slit, loving her with his tongue.

He slid one finger into her hot core. So damn tight. The thought of her wrapping around him made him almost spend. The fear that he would hurt her spiked fear in his soul and he worked her into a fervor, needing her to be ready, to be wet, out of her mind with need before he claimed her virtue.

It did not take her long to relax, to lift her taut ass off the bed, and undulate against his mouth. He held her there, bringing her closer and closer to release, but never quite giving her what she wanted.

"Sebastian, please," she moaned when he flicked her nubbin with his tongue before giving her one last kiss. He came back over her, settled between her legs, and thrust into her core, taking her virginity.

She stilled beneath him, and he stopped moving, giving her time to adjust. He swallowed hard. The urge to take, to satisfy himself, bore down on him. "I'm sorry, my darling. It'll only hurt for a moment or two. I promise."

With the slightest nod, he felt her relax with each breath, and with the slowest, most excruciating thrusts he'd ever known, he started to make love to her while she adjusted to his size.

It didn't take long before she had grown used to him, was moving with her own rhythm. She lifted her legs, clamping them about his hips, and pleasure licked up his spine, hot and demanding.

"Harder, Sebastian," she gasped, her hands clutching his shoulders. He kissed her neck, pumped into her, taking her as she wanted. It was all the approval he needed to increase his pace, give them both what they craved.

He claimed her with abandon, reached down, lifted her bottom. She moaned, and he could feel her tighten about his cock. So good. So damn tight that he was sure he would see stars. Her core pulled at him, and then she broke.

"Sebastian," she cried, clutching at him as he continued to give her what she wanted. What they both needed. Her climax brought on his own, and he came, deep and long. Allowed himself his release to spill into the first woman ever in his life.

He cried out her name, kissing her as his orgasm licked up his spine and didn't seem to abate.

Sebastian breathed deep, trying to calm his racing heart. Damn, he'd never come so hard, gained such pleasure before in the bed of a woman. But this was not any woman. This was his wife.

He lay beside her, pulling her into the crook of his arm before kissing her fiery-red hair. "Are you well? I hope I did not hurt you too much."

She rolled against him, running her hand idly over his chest. "No, ye dinna hurt me at all." She met his gaze, touching her palm to his cheek. "I cannot believe we're married in the truest sense now." She kissed his chest, her lips skimming his flesh and tickling him somewhat.

"You do not regret your choice?" he asked her, needing to

reassure himself he was who she wanted. An absurd reaction considering what they had just done, but he could not help himself. Their union had been so fast, not that he regretted a second of it, but he hoped that she would not. Not ever, if he could help it.

"No, of course not," she replied. "I couldn't be happier to be your wife."

"I am glad," he replied, leaning down to kiss her sweet lips that he doubted he would ever tire of. "Because I'm so happy that I'm your husband." The words truer than he ever thought possible, especially since he'd courted her for one reason and one reason only; what she brought to the marriage.

Not anymore. His ancestral childhood home he cared little for, he realized. So long as the woman in his arms was his, he was home wherever she was, and if that so happened to be at Halligale, then all the better.

CHAPTER 14

Three days later, after telling her friends in Edinburgh her great news, they were on their way south and toward Moy Castle, her childhood home. Julia and Georgina were beyond thrilled by her marriage, if not somewhat put out about her eloping. But once Elizabeth had promised them both she would renew her vows after the Season, they were both willing to let the slight go.

They had several hours to go, and having just broken their fast at an inn several miles back, the carriage ride ahead did not seem as long and arduous as it normally would. Not with the handsome gentleman sitting across from her in the vehicle. She watched him read the newspaper, a small frown between his brow, and couldn't quite believe she was married. That this year it had been her turn to find a husband.

As if he sensed her regard, his eyes flicked over the top of the paper and met hers. The heat banked in his deep-blue orbs made her stomach clench in desire. They had barely left each other's sides these past days, and the bedroom even less.

At the time, Elizabeth had thought there may be something wrong with her that she wanted him as much as she did. That every time he threw her a lazy smile, or knowing look, a wink or grin, she was powerless to deny his pull.

They had made love in numerous places in Georgina's home while she was packing her things to leave, some of them long, delectable hours of lovemaking, while others were quick, sinful tidbits that sated her until they came together at night. Some of the things Sebastian had done to her made her wiggle on her chair. She had been so green, so unaware of what could be between a man and a woman.

She was no longer so innocent.

He set his paper down, a lazy smile across his mouth. A mouth that was as wicked as his tongue. "What are you thinking, my Lizzie?"

He had started to call her that. *My Lizzie.* Every time she heard the name, it made her heart flutter and gave her hope that someday there would be an unbreakable love between them. It had not escaped her notice that neither of them spoke of the emotion or the lack of such a declaration. Elizabeth knew in her heart she was well on the way to loving the rogue sitting across from her and giving her one of his wicked come-hither looks that she could never ignore.

But did he love her? She knew he enjoyed her company, had chased her down over the past weeks until she was his wife, so he must like her very much, but was he falling in love with her? That she could not say, but she hoped and dreamed he would and declare his heart soon. She did not want to be the only one in the marriage, falling in love.

"Nothing of importance, merely admiring my handsome husband."

He chuckled a deep, husky sound that promised all sorts of delicious pleasures. He leaned back in his seat, studying her in turn. "The green velvet you have on today makes your eyes look fiercely bright and absolutely stunning."

Warm appreciation thrummed through her at his words. How had she come to be so lucky to have secured his hand? She glanced down at her gown, running her hand along the gold thread at her bodice. "I had it made especially for the Season this year. I'm glad you like it."

"Come here," he said, his eyes darkening with hunger.

Elizabeth moved to sit beside him. The carriage lurched, and she glanced out the window, noting there was still some time to go. Nothing but fields and forest darkened the view.

A light kiss on her neck startled her a moment before she tipped her head to the side and allowed him to continue his seduction.

"Hell, you smell sweet." He reached for her, tilting her to face him. Their gazes collided, and she knew he wanted her. His eyes burned with need and determination.

Heat pooled at her core, and she went to him, kissing him with all the passion she felt. His hands wrenched her onto his lap, jerking her dress to pool at her waist. Cool air kissed her stockinged legs as her body craved his touch.

He wasn't gentle. He ripped open the front falls off his breeches, his hard manhood spilling against her mons. Elizabeth pressed against him, trying to sate the need that coursed through her body. She wanted him, had watched him for hours, and hoped they may come together in the carriage before they reached her childhood home.

It was naughty, wicked fun to be with Sebastian in such a way. They were husband and wife. There was no real harm in them behaving so, even if it was utterly roguish.

He kissed her hard and long, his tongue tangling with hers. He clasped her hips, his fingers biting into the velvet and her skin beneath. Elizabeth wrapped her arms about his neck, using her knees to place him at her core, before lowering onto his erection.

They both moaned as he settled inside her, fulfilling her every need. Their lovemaking was frantic and fast, both of them needing to sate themselves of the other. He helped her take her pleasure, rocking onto him, pushing her closer to release. He whispered delicious, naughty things in her ear, his whispered breath sending a shiver of desire down her spine.

"Come for me, my darling. Take your pleasure," he gasped, so hard, so large that she thought she may die of the delight of it all.

She kissed him, took his lips, and claimed him as the first tremors of her release shuddered from her core to spike throughout her person. So good that she wondered how she had lived without such a thing for so many years. If it was better known that a woman could find such pleasure with a man, there would certainly be more weddings or love affairs, Elizabeth was certain.

They stayed locked together, their breathing ragged. Elizabeth wondered after the fact what had possessed her, what had made the truth whisper from her lips, but before she could rip the words back from her mouth, she uttered the three weighty words that changed so many people's lives. Their lives forever.

"I love you, Sebastian."

An awkward silence fell between them. Of all the things he'd expected to fall from Lizzie's lips, it had not been the word love. Even so, the words no longer terrified him as they once would have. In fact, he'd had the opposite reaction, had felt nothing but hope and adoration for the woman in his arms. He'd even tried to form his own lips and tongue around the words himself, but they would not form. They became tangled, muddled, and would not declare themselves to her.

Instead, he opted to kiss her, show her with his body what she meant to him. What her honestly made him feel.

What she made him feel.

Love.

CHAPTER 15

$\mathcal{A}$ few hours later, the carriage rocked to a halt before a dark, stone building that looked like a magnificent fortress. Sebastian jumped down, helping Elizabeth alight, his eyes fixed on her childhood home.

A feminine voice called out Elizabeth's name, and he turned to see the late Duke of Law's daughter, Lady Clara, pull Lizzie into a warm embrace, kissing her cheek. Lizzie seemed pleased to see Lady Clara and held her in turn.

Lady Clara's attention turned toward Sebastian and cooled, became guarded. He steeled himself for the reception he would receive here. Did they suspect his motives? Had rumors of their attachment made it to Moy?

"Lord Hastings, whatever are you doing traveling with Lady Elizabeth?"

Lizzie smiled at her friend, letting go of her ladyship's hand to come back to him, clasping his. "Lady Clara, may I present my husband, Lord Hastings."

He'd never seen Lady Clara without words, but here it was, the first time for everything he supposed. The shock and wariness that entered her eyes did not bode well for their announcement.

"Husband? You're married!"

"Who is married?"

Sebastian bowed as Mr. Stephen Grant came out to join his wife, wrapping his arm about her waist. "Elizabeth is married, Stephen. Did you know?"

He frowned, looking between Lizzie and Sebastian. "No, I did not." He turned that frown on to Elizabeth. "Does your brother know?"

"No," Lizzie said, her voice unfazed, but he could feel the tension in her stance, feel the slight shiver that raked over her skin. He gave her a reassuring squeeze, and she threw him a wobbly smile. "I'm here to tell him."

Lady Clara seemed to shake herself out of her shock and came and gave Elizabeth another hug, kissing him, too, on the cheek. "Congratulations to you both. This is wonderful news."

Lizzie relaxed somewhat at her ladyship's words, but the felicitations did not ring true to Sebastian. "Is Brice home?"

"He's in his office," Mr. Grant said, throwing Elizabeth a small smile.

"Thank ye." She turned to him, taking his hands. "I think I should speak to Brice on my own. It'll be a shock to him to hear this news, and I dinna wish to upset ye by his initial reaction."

There was no way he was allowing Elizabeth to face her brother without him. If the laird jumped to the conclusion that the marriage was for the initial reason it was, he needed to be there to defend himself.

You cannot defend the indefensible.

Sebastian ignored the warning voice in his head. As much as he was relieved to know Halligale was back in his hands, that his children would grow up and inherit the estate, the union between him and Lizzie was so much more than the ancient pile of bricks.

After her declaration of love, the words had been spiraling about in his mind, taunting him to admit what he felt for the woman staring up at him with nothing but affection in her beautiful green eyes.

"No, I shall come with you. Your brother needs to hear from both of us, a united front, husband and wife."

With the slightest of nods, she pulled him forward into the home. The estate rivaled even his in Nottinghamshire. The ancient, medieval wooden beams, the staircase, and entrance to the great hall were enormous. Yet, the house did not feel cold or unwelcoming. Large tapestries and family portraits hung on most walls, roaring fires burned in the grates, and he could hear laughter and a woman's voice somewhere else in the home.

"Brice should be through here," he heard Lizzie tell him as he followed.

Sebastian had never met the Laird Mackintosh, had heard his brother mention him with nothing but loathing and anger after he'd lost Halligale in the card game. The man who met his eyes was not what he expected.

He'd assumed the laird to be similar to him in stature and height. He was wrong. The laird was a behemoth of a man, tall and muscular, a Scottish warrior of years past. Sebastian swallowed, pushing down the fear that the man before him could strike him down with his bare hands, and without much effort.

"Brice." Lizzie walked quickly over to her brother and into the man's open arms. He kissed her crown, holding her a moment before he raised his head and spied him standing in the doorway. He hated to think what the Scot thought of him. Sebastian felt as though he had not measured up to his standard from his cool consideration.

He spoke, his voice deep and commanding. A voice that, when spoken, others listened to. "Who is your guest, Elizabeth?"

She came back over to him, taking his hand and pulling him into the room. Sebastian made certain he put some of the desk between the two of them.

"Brice, I would like to introduce you to my husband, Sebastian Denholm, Earl—"

"Hastings," her brother finished for her, his eyes pinning Sebastian with ire. "Husband?!"

Sebastian did not want to flinch or show any sort of fear before the laird, but his yelling of the word *husband* had been unexpected and did catch him off guard. He pulled Lizzie beside him, holding her close. "That is right, my lord. We were married several days ago in Dalmahoy."

The laird's glower did not bode well, not for either of them. "Ye are the brother to the late Earl Hastings?" he queried, his brogue a lot heavier than his sister's. Sebastian also did not miss the thread of wariness in his tone.

"Yes. Emmett Denholm was my elder brother."

"And ye are in Scotland for the Season, hell-bent on catching my bonny sister's hand in marriage by the looks of it. Why are ye not in England like all the other Englishmen marrying English ladies?"

He shrugged, smiling, knowing that from the tone of Lizzie's brother, he did not like Sebastian at all, or the fact he'd made her his wife. "Is not your wife English, my lord?" he put in, not allowing the continual slights to pass undefended. He would only put up with so much before words had to be said.

The laird's eyes narrowed, and Sebastian wondered how far he could taunt the Scot before he had a solid crack across his jaw. He held no regard for the fiend, not after the laird had stolen Halligale from under his brother's nose when he wasn't in the position to gamble and think straight in the first place. Practically robbing his family of their inheritance, their land. If the laird thought he would bow down to his supposed superiority, he was delusional.

"And ye married my sister without my consent, without marriage contracts being signed. Where is the paperwork, Elizabeth?" the laird said, not sparing Elizabeth a whisp of a look, his eyes pinning Sebastian to the spot.

Sebastian choked on his words, having not expected the Scotsman to be so cold. He met Lizzie's eyes and found them wide with alarm. "Brice, I'm not sure I appreciate yer tone. Lord Hastings is my husband. I'm Lady Hastings now. Do not be so cutting and rude."

The laird looked at him, nonplussed, seemingly ignoring his sister's words. "And I'm not sure if I appreciate ye marrying a rogue we dinna know much about, other than the fact he's the brother to a man I trusted less than the Jacobite army trusted King Charles II."

"Brice," Elizabeth gasped, glaring up at her brother. She had mettle, his wife. Few would look up at such a giant of a man and chastise him. "I shall tell Sophie what a beast you're being, and then you may realize your mistake."

The laird crossed his arms over his chest. "Ye will do no such thing. Ye know Sophie is unwell and needs rest. She's not to be troubled with this dilemma you've tangled yourself into. I shall deal with this false marriage and extradite ye from it."

"You will not." Lizzie took a step forward, using the desk to lean on and press her point. "The marriage is consummated. There were witnesses and a reverend. There is nothing ye can do to change the course of my life. I married the man I love, and I shall remain so no matter the reason ye dislike him so much."

"Mayhap ye would like to know, sister, where my dislike comes from." the laird said, a muscle working in his jaw.

Dread coiled in Sebastian's stomach. This was the moment he had been dreading. If Elizabeth found out the truth as it once had stood, she would never forgive him. He would lose her.

"Come, Elizabeth," he said, clasping her hand and trying to drag her from the room. "We shall return to England. Maybe in time, Laird Mackintosh will cool his ire and think more clearly and fairly regarding our union."

"Unlikely," the laird said, glaring at him. The laird turned to his sister. "Come, Elizabeth, we need to speak, and alone. Ye deserve to know the truth."

"Pardon," she said, clearly confused. "What on earth has ye like this, Brice? I dinna understand."

The laird, instead of coming over to Sebastian, taking him by his shoulders and hoisting him back out into the hall, he walked about his desk, sitting as if he had not a care in the world. "Sit, ye will need to be off ye feet when ye hear what I have to say."

Lizzie threw him a cautious look, and Sebastian knew she was fearful of what her brother knew, and she did not. What Sebastian had possibly kept from her that would have changed her opinion of him. Kept her from marrying him.

The thought he could lose her in a matter of minutes sent panic to coil through his gut, and he fought not to sweat. He sat beside Lizzie, taking her hand in the hopes to calm her when she learned of his brother and her inheritance.

The laird sighed, rubbing a hand across his jaw. "I knew the late Lord Hastings. In fact, when he was here the Season before last, I ran into him in Edinburgh while up there on business. A game of cards was played, Lord Hastings was a terrible gambler and lost often, and yet, it dinna stop him from being a fool and thinking that was not the case."

Lizzie squeezed his hand, throwing him a concerned glance. "I'm sorry your brother was troubled, Sebastian."

He raised her hand, kissing it. "It has nothing to do with us, my dear. Do not concern yourself with my sibling."

"Even so, I'm sorry."

His heart thumped hard in his chest that she was worried for him. That she cared. Sebastian met the laird's hard gaze and prepared himself for the axe to fall across his neck.

"The late Lord Hastings, low on funds, opted to gamble his Scottish family estate. A house that his mother had inherited not long after her marriage. The estate that I gifted ye, Elizabeth."

Sebastian took a moment to steel himself before he could bring himself to meet Elizabeth's startled eyes. That she had taken but moments to understand what her brother was saying said a lot about her intelligence. Her eyes filled with tears and his heart crumbled in his chest. He reached for her, but she wrenched away, standing and moving over toward the desk.

"You married me to gain back ye family estate?" She paused a moment, swallowing hard. "Is that what ye did, Sebastian?"

He shook his head, standing. "No, I did not."

The laird growled, literally growled. "Dinna make a fool of my sister a second time, Lord Hastings. Own the truth and shame the devil, boy."

"I am not a boy, and you'll be best to remember that," Sebastian roared, having about enough of being treated like the worst person on the planet. "At first, I may have seen the opportunity, Lizzie, but it has since become so much more than an estate. I love you as much as you love me. I no longer care about Halligale."

"You're a liar. Ye courted me, pursued me and no one else, and the stupid, blind fool that I was imagined it to be because ye truly wanted me. Wanted no one else but me, but all ye wanted was what I bought to the marriage."

Sebastian held up his hands, hoping to make her understand. "I admit, I came to Scotland to try to gain Halligale back in some way. When I found out that you had been given the estate, my mind, of course, came to the conclusion that a union with you would be the easiest course. I could have simply asked to purchase it back, Lizzie, but I did not. Not because I couldn't afford the estate, but because once I got to know you, I found you were a gift that I had not thought to receive. I fell in love with you and your sweet nature. I no longer care for the estate. I want you."

"Really," she said, her tone one of disbelief. "Then, when I sign the house back over to my brother, removing ye from gaining the estate, ye will still profess your love. Still wish to remain married to me."

"Of course," he said, knowing that such a transaction would be impossible. She was his wife now. What was hers was his by law. "Forget what we bring to the marriage, and please remember what we're like together. How much you love me. How much I love you."

CHAPTER 16

*H*ow much she loved him? Elizabeth almost scoffed at the absurd notion. She had been played the fool, and she had been the only one who had not known it. How many other people attending the Scottish Season knew Lord Hasting was there with an ulterior motive? To marry her and gain his ancestral home back.

What a slimly, English bastard.

"How dare ye? I was the laughingstock of London before, and now ye have made me so a second time. I shall never live down the shame of marrying a man who tricked me into the union simply to gain his old estate back. It will not be you, an earl, who'll suffer the snide remarks and snickering giggles as ye walk past. Oh no, they will be reserved solely for me."

"No one will say such things, Lizzie. I shall not allow it, and it is not true."

"That is absolute horse dung, Sebastian." She paced away from him, a fury running hot through her blood. "That you say ye no longer care what happens to the estate is also a lie. You care, quite a lot, and it was why ye were so keen on an elopement so soon into our courtship.

Ye did not want me to form any affections with anyone else. Ye have taken from me the ability to make a match with solid foundations. Your love is a pack of cards similar to your brother's, which were destined to crumble."

He ran a hand through his hair, and she could see the frustration thrumming through his body. "Yes, I did court you originally to regain the house, but it was days only before that all changed. I want you, Lizzie. And no matter what your brother says," he said, pointing to Brice, "what I feel for you is stronger than anything I've ever experienced before. I have never told a woman that I love her. And I do love you so much. I do not want to lose you."

"And yet ye will for you are the worst of what lives beyond the Scottish border. A selfish, self-serving Englishman who dinna care for anything or anyone except himself."

Her brother grunted his approval to his sister's words.

"You stay out of this argument. This is not your battle." Sebastian pointed at the laird, glaring at the bastard.

The laird stood, his chair scraping on the wooden floor. "Ye best stop talking now, Lord Hastings."

Sebastian heard the warning in his tone, but he refused to listen, to concede. He needed Lizzie to believe him. To love him and be with him as she'd promised she would. He could not lose her now. Not for this reason, not when that reason no longer mattered to him.

"Make me," he said, prepared to defend himself, defend his future with Lizzie.

"Enough!" Elizabeth's voice cut between them, pulling Sebastian out of his impending thrashing with the Laird

Mackintosh. "Brice, please give me a moment with Sebastian."

Her brother glared at him one last moment before he stormed from the room, the door slamming hard behind him.

Sebastian did not move, scared that if he did, she would bolt, and his chance of explaining, of getting her to understand, would be over. "Lizzie, please try to see the situation from my side. I did not mean to hurt you."

"No, I suppose you did not. You did not expect me to find out. A stupid assumption considering who my brother is and his association with yours. What made you think that you would not be called out for your shady actions?"

Before he had a chance to answer, she waved his words aside. "You never thought to not get away with it, did you? You knew my brother would make the connection, see your reasons for marrying me, and call you out on it. But if I was already married to you, the marriage consummated, well, there would be naught my brother or anyone could do to undo our union."

When put like that, Sebastian could see he looked like a right bastard. He had pushed her quicker than he ought, needed their marriage watertight before he met her brother. What she said was true, and he could not defend himself against the charge.

Even if he now loved her, wanted her above anything else in the world, his words would fall unheard by her, for he'd ruined what chance they had by being dishonest.

"For what it is worth, I do love you, Lizzie. I may not have set out with honorable intentions, but for me, I have long thought of no other than you. I want our marriage to be a happy one. Please forgive me."

She shook her head, anger all but thrumming through her. "No, I cannot. Ye are not to be trusted. You're a liar, a thief dressed in fine, superfine coats and polished hessian boots. I want nothing to do with ye." She strode over to the desk, scribbling on a piece of parchment before folding it and flicking it to the edge of the desk.

"What is this?" he asked, picking it up.

"Give the note to Mrs. Gardener at Halligale. She knows my signature and will believe that you're my husband. You wanted the estate back, well, now ye have it. I hope ye enjoy your pile of bricks."

"Lizzie, the home was my mother's. The one place that all my happy memories were made. Please do not do this."

"Get out," she said, her voice hard and brooking no argument. "We shall remain married because I cannae change that fact, but know, from this day forward, we're no longer husband and wife. I dinna want anything to do with ye."

Sebastian debated going around the desk and taking her in his arms, holding her and trying to push his reasoning. But her eyes burned with hurt and anger, and he would not force himself on her. He would try again. Another day he would return and attempt to win back her affections.

"I'm sorry," he said, striding from the room and heading straight out the front door. The carriage was unloaded, but he did not miss the fact that his trunks were still tied to the back of the equipage. The laird stood to the side, giving the driver orders, his arms crossed over his sizable chest.

"Ye are to return to England. If I hear of ye going to Halligale, I shall have ye disposed of where no one will hear from ye again. Dinna think just because ye are my sister's husband that I'll forgive ye for tricking her into marriage so to gain her estate. Ye are never to set foot here again, or anywhere near Halligale."

"I own the estate beside Lizzie's, and I shall return there if I wish. Not you or anyone will tell me what I can and cannot do."

The laird's mouth curled up into a snarl. "Obviously, you do whatever ye want and dinna care for the consequences."

Sebastian turned and climbed up into the carriage. He ignored the laird who stood in front of the home as if to keep him at bay. He scanned the windows, wishing to see Lizzie, even if for one last time. He did not know when he would see her, and the thought of never seeing her again made him want to cast up his accounts.

No, this was not the end, not their friendship or marriage. She loved him as much as he loved her. What did it matter that he happened to fall in love with the woman who had inherited his ancestral home?

You did not tell her the truth, and that is the problem.

He closed his eyes a moment as the carriage lurched forward. It did not matter, and yet that was all that mattered, really. He had not been honest, and in by doing so, by setting out to first deceive, he had ruined any chance for them.

He glanced back at the house, despair clasping his chest when he found the windows empty of her—his Lizzie.

CHAPTER 17

*E*lizabeth stayed at Moy Castle for the night before heading to the estate her brother had gifted her. A home she had come to love but now was no longer so sure she wished to keep. She could sell it, she supposed. Her brother had mentioned the option if she could not bear to keep it.

The carriage rolled to a stop before Halligale, a rambling and whimsical home she'd come to love. She jumped down without waiting for assistance and looked up at the estate. Her mind, try as she might, could not help but imagine Sebastian here as a child. Running about the large home, the manicured gardens, being chased by his brother, nanny, or mother.

She had not been listening to him as much as she should have, she supposed. As a woman who came from a loving family—her brother, at least—she could understand Sebastian wishing to gain his estate back. The one place he had the happiest memories of childhood.

Sighing, she headed inside. The housekeeper greeted her in the foyer. Elizabeth ordered a bath and the fire to be lit in her room, exhaustion nipping at her heels. After her travels these past days, and the emotional toll that accompanied her, all she wished for was a relaxing bath and sleep.

To be alone and sort out her life, what she would do, how she could move forward with the truth she now had to live with.

Her room was just as she remembered it, warm and welcoming, the light drapes and bedding giving the space a feminine feel and lighting up the dark-timbered woods. She sat on the edge of the bed, watched as the maid fussed about with her trunks and gowns, a scullery maid working hard to light a fire in the grate.

"Would ye care for ye dinner to be served, Lady Elizabeth?"

She nodded, ignoring the fact they were still calling her by her unmarried name. Of course, they would. They did not know that she had been married, and was now the wife of Earl Hastings. A countess.

"I will have it in here in an hour. Thank ye," she said, not wanting to use the dining room.

Two footmen carried up a copper bath and set it before the hearth before a whole line of servants brought up bucket after bucket of water. Her bath was soothing, relieved her aching bones, and relaxed her for the first time in two days.

As she climbed into bed later that night, she couldn't help but wonder where Sebastian was. Had he returned to London? Was he at his new estate next door, or was he in Edinburgh? A small part of her hoped he was at Bragdon Manor so she may see him, have him explain to her yet again what his reasoning was to break her heart. Anything to make her understand, to believe that she had not been duped into marriage all for the sake of a house.

. . .

*D*ays passed, and she had been back at Halligale for almost a week when Julia descended from Edinburgh to visit her. Elizabeth poured them tea in the downstairs drawing room. She had not written to her friends telling them of her pain, her situation as it stood with Sebastian. So why was Julia here? She was curious to find out.

Julia held her tea in her hands, her attention traveling over Elizabeth and not missing one detail. Thankfully her friend was polite enough not to mention the dark shadows beneath her eyes or that she had lost weight and none of her gowns fit her properly anymore.

"Georgina and I had a visit from Lord Hastings several days ago," she said matter-of-fact. "He suggested that we travel down to Moy Castle and see you. Georgina could not get away from Edinburgh, but I came, only to find that you had decamped from Moy and were back at Halligale. I'm glad to find you at home here."

Her friend's guarded words put her on edge. She sipped her tea, studying Julia. Whatever had her friend heard? That Sebastian had gone and seen them, well, she wasn't sure what she thought of that. If he thought involving her friends, getting them to side with him would help his cause, he was delusional.

"Sebastian visited ye. I suppose ye were surprised to see him and without me in attendance."

"We were both surprised, and before you ask, no, he did not say why we should come here and see ye, only that he was concerned and thought ye may need a friend."

Elizabeth bit the inside of her mouth, fighting off a flow of tears that up until right now she'd been able to blink away. She would not cry. She would not allow anyone to make her succumb to tears again. After her embarrassment in London

—Lucky Lizzie—she had sworn never to cry over trivial things.

This is hardly insignificant, Elizabeth.

She stared down at her hands, at the wedding ring that now circled one finger like a beacon of her failure. "Lord Hastings married me because this house that we now sit in was his childhood home. His brother lost it in a game of cards to my brother two years ago, or thereabouts. I was his means of getting it back."

Julia's mouth gaped, and for several moments she did not speak at all. Elizabeth shoved away from the embarrassment that wanted to swamp her. This was not her fault. This was Sebastian's fault. He was the bastard who had set out with this plan. She had been merely the innocent party in the affair.

"Lord Hastings did what?" Julia's teacup rattled on its plate, and she set it down with a clank. "He told ye this?"

Elizabeth nodded. "He did, yes. When we traveled to Moy, my brother made the connection and saw through his marriage to me. Sebastian could not deny it, tried to make me see the reasoning as to why he did what he did. I still cannot believe it myself." Elizabeth stood, walking over to the window and looking out over the estate. The grounds that Sebastian thought more of than she did. "He grew up here with his mother, who was Scottish. A lot of happy memories, so it would seem. An ancestral home he was loath to lose and therefore thought to trick me into marriage as an easier way in which to get it back."

"But surely," Julia said beseechingly. "He loves ye. I'm certain of it. Is there a chance that he fell in love with ye during his courting of ye as well? And so, his fixation on the estate shifted to ye, and the home became secondary. I simply cannot believe any man could treat a woman with so little respect. I cannot believe it of him. It is too awful."

Elizabeth shrugged, unable to turn and face her friend. "That is what he says. He says that he fell in love with me while working toward his original plan, but I cannot suppose that." Or perhaps she did, but she could not forgive him for his treachery. That all those sweet words, the long considerations across a ballroom floor, the waltzes they had shared had all been a ploy, a game for him to see how hard it would be for her to fall at his feet.

Heat rushed her cheeks. She had been uncommonly easy to form an attachment, had barely given anyone else a chance after Lord Hastings had started to follow her skirts about town. What a mindless fool she had been. What a cad he had been in turn.

"He looked wretched when he came to see us, Elizabeth, as if he had hardly slept."

"Good," she spat, harsher than she ought. Julia did not deserve her wrath, her disappointment in Sebastian. "I'm sorry. Please know I'm not angry at ye."

Julia came and joined her at the window. "Know that I'm on your side, and I shall defend and support ye to the bitter end if that is what you wish of me, but before you make any hasty decisions, ye must think on this. There is the possibility that Lord Hastings may have started out with underhanded intentions, but that they were soon scuttled when yer charm and warmth, and it caught him unawares. He loves ye, does he not?" Julia asked.

Elizabeth nodded once. "So he declares."

Julia clasped her hands, shaking them a little to gain her attention. "Ye are loveable, Elizabeth. No matter what nickname London termed you. Lord Hastings ignored all that, he came to know ye, the real ye, and he fell in love with that woman. If he did not care, he would not have come back to Edinburgh to your friends and beg them to go to Moy. He would have turned about, traveled to London, and set his lawyers for Scotland to gain back this estate."

"There is still time. He may have already done such a thing for all that I know."

"He was still in Edinburgh when I left."

Elizabeth did not know what to think. Over the past days, her emotions had experienced a range of highs and lows. Of hope and despair. It was no surprise he had not chased her down to Halligale after she had told him she did not wish to see him again. But she knew she needed to take Julia's words into consideration. People do change. Was it possible that Sebastian had done so?

"When people find out that I inherited Halligale and that the previous family who owned it is none other than my new husband, there will be talk. I'll be ridiculed at every party I attend, pitied because people will think Sebastian married me for his lost estate."

"They may say such things," Julia agreed. "But after years of a happy marriage, of children and love, Elizabeth, what can they say after that?" Julia smiled. "They will say they were wrong, and ye can make them eat their words. Ye can live a happy marriage and not care what their opinion is."

For the first time in what felt like weeks, she smiled. Julia was so very smart and insightful. When one was melancholy and unable to see straight through their pain, she was always the one friend who was honest and offered a different point of view.

Not that Elizabeth had not been hoping, wondering the same thing, but it was nice to hear it from someone else all the same.

She would face talk, snickers, and giggles as she walked by, reactions she had come to loathe after her embarrassing Season, but she could survive it. With Sebastian by her side, with his support and love, she could sustain anything.

"I need time to think all of this through, to decide what I wish to do." Elizabeth pulled Julia into a quick embrace. "Thank ye for coming down here to see me. To tell me what ye have. You are the best of friends."

"I want ye to be happy, Elizabeth, and something tells me that yer heart too was touched with Lord Hastings. Without him, I fear you will never be content. Think about everything I said, decide your path. As I declared earlier, Georgina and I will be there for ye, no matter your choice."

"Thank ye," she said, more grateful than Julia would ever know for her insight. "I know that ye do."

*Sebastian could not stay in Edinburgh long. The Season held no appeal for him or the city now that Elizabeth was not within its walls. He traveled down to Bragdon Manor, took daily walks, and thought over how he could win her back.

So far, he'd failed at the task. Any way he looked at his predicament, a solution, nothing proved he loved her more than the estate.

The way he set out to win Elizabeth had been wrong, ungentlemanly, and cruel. Of course, he'd never meant for her to find out. That idea more than imperative after he realized he was falling in love with her.

A foolish ideal that would never happen. Not with her brother knowing the truth and seeing his motives.

Now that she did know his motives, he would forever be frowned upon in her family if he ever came within a foot of them again. After the laird's dismissal of him, Elizabeth's too, he doubted that would ever occur.

"Damn it all to hell." He swiped a long stick he held in his hand over the tall grass he was walking through on the boundary of his estate and Elizabeth's. He'd found out by a footman that she was in residence there, alone. Her friend Lady Julia had visited last week but had returned to town after staying but a few days.

He stopped, staring over toward his childhood home, watching as the afternoon sun made the west-facing windows reflect the golden rays. Several chimneys bore smoke, a homely, welcoming place he had to admit he no longer cared too much about.

What he cared about was the woman who sat within its walls. What was she thinking? Had she calmed down somewhat after the explosive truth had ruined what had been between them? He did not know, and right at this moment, he was too fearful of finding out. The fear of her reaction of her pushing him away a second time made him want to cast up his accounts. How on earth could he make her see he loved her? Truly loved her and not her inheritance.

A twig cracked somewhere to his right, and he turned to see the startled face of Elizabeth, her bonnet hanging idly in her hand by a blue ribbon. Her light-blue afternoon gown made his heart stutter in his chest.

Hell, he'd missed her. Her beauty, hair hanging loose over her shoulders, held off her face by a few pins, her green eyes wide with shock at seeing him again. He stared at her for a long moment, captivated by her charm. "Lizzie," he said at length, not moving for fear she'd bolt.

"You're at Bragdon Manor?" she asked, glancing quickly toward his estate.

"I am, but not for long. I'm having my things packed and readied for transport to England. I'm selling the property and going back to Nottinghamshire." Lizzie did not deserve to have him living near her in Scotland, certainly if she did not wish him to be near her again. He would honor her wish, give her what she wanted and live in the hope that one day she would forgive him and return to his arms.

"Oh." Was all she said, nodding slightly. "I suppose since the law states what is mine is yours, you have your ancestral home back and do not need two estates side by side."

"That is not why I'm selling," he corrected her, hating that she believed what was no longer true. Had not been the truth for him for several weeks. "I do not want Halligale either. You can do whatever you want with the estate. I shall not stand in your way."

"Really." The word was curt and held an edge of suspicion to it. As if she did not believe a word he said.

The one way he could prove he did not care about the estate was to leave, go back to England, and continue his married life alone. "What I say is the truth, Lizzie. I no longer want Halligale, for I've come to understand that it has to hold those you love within it for a house to be home." He took a cautious step toward her, and yet she stepped back, out of his reach. "I could take the estate, live there, but I would not be as happy as I was as a child, for you would not be there with me. In gaining the estate, I would lose you, and nothing is worth that."

She studied him a moment, but he could see she was unsure of his words. Distrusted him. Would he ever earn her trust again, relish in her love and warmth once more? Hell, he hoped he did.

"I know you do not believe me, and that is why I'm going. I cannot change our situation. We're married, and there is no undoing that." He shrugged. "This is the only way in which to think to prove myself to you. To leave, but know," he said, trying to take her hands and failing a second time, "I do love you, Lizzie. Somewhere in my grand plan of gaining back what was mine, I captured something so much more precious."

She swallowed, her eyes glassy and bright. "And what was that, Lord Hastings?"

He flinched at the use of his title, but what did he expect? He'd lost the right for her to call him Sebastian. Husband. Lover.

"Your heart." This time, Sebastian clasped her upper arms and kissed her quickly on the cheek before turning and striding away. This was for the best. He could not stay. To do so may push her further away. If he had any chance of winning her back, England was where he had to decamp. Wait and hope she would one day arrive on his front step.

Ready to claim what will always be hers.

His love.

CHAPTER 18

*T*hree months passed and what Sebastian had told her the day out on the heather-strewn land, that he was leaving, still held true. He had not come back to Scotland in all that time, had remained at his estate in Nottinghamshire. What town gossip she did receive from family and friends in England stated, in any case.

From all accounts, the once rakehell, most sought-after bachelor in London had eschewed the city's delights and secluded himself away at his country estate. She had not believed he would sell the estate next door, but within weeks the home was sold, and the new owners were already living in and enjoying their Scottish abode.

When the home had sold, and news reached her that Sebastian was safely back in England, and the distance gnawed at her like a cancerous tumor.

As the weeks turned into months, his absence weighed her down, and for the past few weeks, she had started to look at her situation a lot more clearly. See past her initial anger and disappointment and understand why he'd done what he had.

He may not have banked on falling in love with her, but he did, and she now believed that more than anything else. She had visited Moy several weeks into his departure and found out Sebastian had signed over any claim to Halligale. If she wished to, she could sell the estate and be done with the connection, but no matter how mad he had made her, she could not do that to him.

The estate had been his childhood home. The very walls, rooms and gardens she had come to love, she adored even more because of the boy who grew up within its stone and mortar.

She could not sell it just to prove that he loved her.

His leaving, giving up of the home, the despair she had read in his eyes the day out on the land when their paths crossed, told her his affections toward her were true.

He loved her. Had fallen in love with her despite his initial plan, and if it were the estate she had inherited that had brought about that love, then she would cherish the house forever.

The carriage turned into the gates of Wellsworth Abbey, and Elizabeth moved to look out the window at the large Georgian mansion that was Sebastian's English estate.

It was more formal than the wild, rugged one his mother had owned, and yet it was just as beautiful. Nerves tumbled in her stomach at the thought of seeing him again after so many months. Would he admit her? Did he still love her?

Elizabeth knew to the core of her being she loved him. Had missed him, no matter how much she may have tried not to at the beginning of their separation.

Their estrangement, no matter how painful, was required, however. She needed time to think, time to heal, and move past her hurt. To forgive him.

The carriage rocked to a halt, and a footman bounded up to the vehicle, opening the door. Elizabeth stepped down, stretching out the soreness in her bones that miles of travel had wrought on her body.

A gentleman rounded the corner of the house, his attention on the paperwork in his hands, his head down, and not looking where he was going.

Warmth ran through her like whisky at the sight of Sebastian. He was dressed in tan breeches and black hessian boots that were covered with dust. A shirt and waistcoat, no jacket, and the sleeves of his shirt were rolled up to his elbows. Had he been out and about the estate, looking in on his tenant farms, the fields?

As if sensing company, he glanced up and skidded to a stop, his eyes darting from her to the carriage and the abundant of traveling trunks stacked on the back of the vehicle.

"Hello, husband. Are ye not going to greet me?" she asked him, amused somewhat by his shock.

"Lizzie?" Her name came out with an exhaled breath, and her heart pinched at the disbelief that ran through his tone.

He had not thought she would come. Perhaps he never thought to see her again. Silly man. When women were angry, and especially Scottish women, one must understand that time is required to forgive and move forward in life.

She stepped toward him, smiling. "Sebastian. Ye look well," she said, aware that they were being watched by an abundance of staff.

"I am as good as I can be." He frowned, taking in her wrinkled gown, and Elizabeth knew she had several strands of hair loose about her face.

"You must be tired." He clasped her hand, kissing it. Without letting her go, he turned for the door, barking out orders for her trunks to be unpacked in the countess's rooms beside his own.

"Come, we can speak in my library."

Elizabeth followed him, taking in his home. Marble

floors, family portraits, and rich tapestries hung on the walls. Dark-chestnut doors led into numerous rooms. She saw little of them before she was rushed into the library, where he closed and locked the door.

She strolled over to the fire, warming her sore muscles. She turned and found him staring at her with something akin to disbelief.

"Ye did not expect me," she stated, knowing that after months of separation, not many people would, certainly not after the way they parted.

A small frown set between his brows, and Elizabeth had the overwhelming desire to wipe it away, to take away his fear. "I did not think I would ever see you again. It has been so long."

He moved toward her, but not close enough that she could reach out and touch him.

"Our separation has given me time to think, Sebastian." She unhooked her pelisse, throwing it over a nearby wing-back chair. "And while I dinna agree with how ye set out to win my hand, I am not unhappy that we're married. Not anymore."

She closed the space between them, staring up at him. He looked good enough to devour. His eyes burned with hope and fear both. His slightly disheveled appearance gave him an air of ruggedness that she liked. Not so much the lord of the manor, but a man, delightful, strong, husband of hers.

"You do not regret being my wife?"

She shook her head. "No. I want to be yer wife."

He reached out, clasping her hands. "But what about what I did to you? How I tricked you into marrying me?"

"Well, the fact that fate had you falling in love with the woman ye set out to fool, I consider myself the victor in this, for you are mine to command. Mine to love."

"I am yours," he declared, kissing both her hands in turn.

"I'm sorry, Lizzie. I have missed you so much." He pulled her against him, holding her tight in arms that locked about her, like an impenetrable band.

"When my brother told me ye had signed any rights of Halligale over to me, I knew that ye loved me, for I knew how much that house meant to ye."

"It means nothing to me without you in my life." He reached up, pushing the loose strands of hair away from her face, his thumbs idly sliding over her cheeks. "I have missed you so much."

She blinked back tears. They could move forward, have a life together, a marriage. "I missed ye too. Once I decided to forgive ye your stupidity."

His lips twitched. Oh, she'd missed him, everything about the man in her arms. Even if he had been absurdly stupid, to begin with. "Are you here to stay with me?"

"I am," she said, looking about the room. "And when ye want, we can travel to Scotland to your home there as well. I want ye in my life, Sebastian, and from this day forward, I never wish to be parted from ye again."

"I love you. So much." He wrapped her in his arms a second time before pulling back and taking her lips in a searing kiss. Her body heated, liquified at the feel of him again, his warmth, the commanding way he took her mouth.

It did not take long for the kiss to turn from beckoning and sweet to hot and needy. The months apart acted as a kaleidoscope of need. Elizabeth wrapped her arms around his neck, kissing him back with undisguised desire.

His hands were everywhere, teasing and touching, stroking and tweaking. She moaned when one hand covered her breast, rolling her nipple between his fingers.

"I want you," he gasped, bending to scoop her into his arms. He carried her over toward the fire, laying her down on the thick Aubusson rug beneath them. And then he was atop her. His powerful body settling between her legs, atop her chest.

Lizzie reached down, fumbling with the buttons on his breeches. One of his hands supported his weight, the other making quick work of her gown, wrenching it above her hips. He thrust into her, taking her with hard, deep strokes. She sighed. This was right, what she wanted. Had missed so very much.

Lizzie wrapped her legs about his hips, letting go and giving over to his desire, the desperation in each thrust, each touch, and kiss he bestowed on her. She ran her hand through his hair, clasping his nape, trying to calm him.

"I'm not going anywhere, Sebastian," she said, slowing their kiss. "Not ever again."

He quieted his lovemaking, and it was more devastating than anything she had ever known. In every kiss, every touch, she could feel the reverence he felt for her, the care and love he had.

"I love you, my darling wife."

She arched her back, enjoying this newfound pace particularly. "I love ye too. Now and forever."

"Yes. Now and forever."

EPILOGUE

Halligale Estate, 1813 Scotland

Sebastian threw his son in the air, catching him as he giggled and screamed at the game. He was a strapping lad, already a young hellion and a handful for his mother. Ewan Sebastian Brice Denholm, Viscount Trent, future Earl Hastings, was the most perfect boy. Watching him stumble and run to his mama made Sebastian's heart twist in his chest.

Lizzie and Ewan were everything to him, and every day he thanked the stars in the heavens he had not lost his wife due to his own foolish actions.

"Stop throwing him in the air, Sebastian," she said, setting their boy back on his feet and watching as he ran back to him. "He'll be sick all over himself before Brice and Sophie arrive."

Sebastian inwardly groaned, seating himself on a nearby settee, content to watch his son pick up and play with the wooden blocks at his feet. Brice had eventually forgiven him for his conduct, but it had taken two years after their reunion. Still, even to this day, three years into their marriage, he sometimes wondered if the Scottish laird believed he loved his sister.

Not that he cared what Laird Mackintosh thought, so long as Lizzie loved him, that was all that mattered.

"He likes being thrown in the air. He will not be sick. He's too tough for that nonsense."

Right at that moment, his son coughed, spitting up some of his lunch over the front of his clothing. Lizzie threw him a knowing *I told you so* look and called for his nurse.

"No, I shall take him up and change him." He scooped his son up in his arms, leaning down to kiss his wife as he walked past. "I shall not be long."

"Good." she grinned up at him, laughing when Ewan reached for her face, kissing her cheek. "Thank you, my darling boy," she said, kissing him back.

Sebastian chuckled, pulling their son away.

He did not think he could have been any happier than the day she arrived at his estate, forgiveness in her heart, but he was wrong. Right now, every day since that day. had been better than the last.

The birth of their first child, her body rounding again with their second. Hell, he prayed for a girl, a wee lass with fiery red hair and brilliant, green eyes just like her mama. Their life was perfect, happy, and blissful.

When his brother had lost the estate, and he had set out to win the woman who inherited it, little did he know how much he owed his foolish sibling. He owed him his life. His happiness.

"Darling," Lizzie called as he started out the drawing room door.

"Yes?" He turned to her, counting down the hours until he had her in his arms once again. Alone in their room.

Her eyes warmed as if she knew what he was thinking.

Understood the secrets of his heart. "Nothing really, only that I love ye."

He winked, tickling his lad when he wiggled on his shoulder, letting out a squeal of laughter for his efforts. "I adore you too," he replied to her. Reveling in her beauty and the love that shone from her eyes. And he always would.

His own perfect Highland Rose.

Thank you for taking the time to read *To Kiss a Highland Rose*! I hope you enjoyed the sixth book in my Kiss the Wallflower series.

I'm forever grateful to my readers, so if you're able, I would appreciate an honest review of *To Kiss a Highland Rose*. As they say, feed an author, leave a review! You can contact me at tamaragillauthor@gmail.com or sign up to my newsletter to keep up with my writing news.

If you'd like to learn about book one in my To Marry a Rogue series, *Only an Earl Will Do*, please read on. I have included the prologue for your reading pleasure.

ONLY AN EARL WILL DO

TO MARRY A ROGUE, BOOK 1

The reigning queen of London society, Lady Elizabeth Worthingham, has her future set out for her. Marry well, and marry without love. An easy promise to make and one she owed her family after her near ruinous past that threatened them all. And the rakish scoundrel Henry Andrews, Earl of Muir who's inability to act a gentleman when she needed one most would one day pay for his treachery.

. . .

Returning to England after three years abroad, Henry is determined to make the only woman who captured his heart his wife. But the icy reception he receives from Elizabeth is colder than his home in the Scottish highlands. As past hurts surface and deception runs as thick as blood, so too does a love that will overcome all obstacles, unless a nameless foe, determined with his own path, gets his way and their love never sees the light of day...

PROLOGUE

England 1805 – Surrey

"You're ruined."

Elizabeth stood motionless as her mother, the Duchess of Penworth, paced before the lit hearth, her golden silk gown billowing out behind her, the deep frown between her eyes daring anyone to follow her. "No. Let me rephrase that. The family is ruined. All my girls, their futures, have been kicked to the curb like some poor street urchins."

Elizabeth, the eldest of all the girls, swiped a lone tear from her cheek and fought not to cast up her accounts. "But surely Henry has written of his return." She turned to her father. "Papa, what did his missive say?" The severe frown lines between her father's brows were deeper than she'd ever seen them before, and dread pooled in her belly. What had she done? What had Henry said?

"I shall not read it to you, Elizabeth, for I fear it'll only upset you more, and being in the delicate condition you are we must keep you well. But never again will I allow the Earl of Muir to step one foot into my home. To think," her father said, kicking at a log beside the fire, "that I supported him to seek out his uncle in America. I'm utterly ashamed of myself."

"No," Elizabeth said, catching her father's gaze. "You have nothing to be ashamed of. I do. I'm the one who lay with a man who wasn't my husband. I'm the one who now carries his child." The tears she'd fought so hard to hold at bay started to run in earnest. "Henry and I were friends, well, I thought we were friends. I assumed he'd do the right thing by our family, by me. Why is it that he'll not return?"

Her mother, quietly staring out the window, turned at her question. "Because his uncle has said no nephew of his would marry a strumpet who gave away the prize before the contracts were signed, and Henry apparently was in agreement with this statement."

Her father sighed. "There is an old rivalry between Henry's uncle and me. We were never friends, even though I noted Henry's father high in my esteem, as close as a brother, in fact. Yet his sibling was temperamental, a jealous cur."

"Why were you not friends with Henry's uncle, Papa?" He did not reply. "Please tell me. I deserve to know."

"Because he wished to marry your mama, and I won her hand instead. He was blind with rage, and it seems even after twenty years he wishes to seek revenge upon me by ruining you."

Elizabeth flopped onto a settee, shocked by such news. "Did Henry know of this between you and his uncle? Did you ever tell him?"

"No. I thought it long forgotten."

Elizabeth swallowed as the room started to swirl. "So, Henry has found his wealthy uncle and has been poisoned by his lies. The man has made me out to be a light-skirts of little character." She took a calming breath. "Tell me, does the letter really declare this to be Henry's opinion as well?"

The duke came and sat beside her. "It is of both their opinions, yes." He took her hand and squeezed it. "You need to marry, Elizabeth, and quickly. There is no other choice."

She stood, reeling away from her father and such an idea. To marry a stranger was worse than no marriage at all and falling from grace. "I cannot do that. I haven't even had a season. I know no one."

"A good friend of mine, Viscount Newland, recently passed. His son, Marcus, who is a little simple of mind after a fall from a horse as a child, is in need of a wife. But because of his ailment, no one will have him. They are desperate to keep the estate within the family and are looking to marry him off. It would be a good match for you both. I know it is not what you wanted, but it will save you and your sisters from ruin."

Elizabeth stood looking down at her father, her mouth agape with shock and not a little amount of disgrace. "You want me to marry a simpleton?"

"His speech is a little delayed only, otherwise he's a kind young man. I grant you he's not as handsome as Henry, but... well, we must do what's best in these situations."

Her mother sighed. "Lord Riddledale has called and asked for your hand once more. You could always accept his suit."

"Please, I would rather cut off my own hand than marry his lordship." Just the thought was enough to make her skin crawl.

"Well then, you will marry Lord Newland. I'm sorry, but it must and will be done," her mother said, her tone hard.

Elizabeth walked to the window that looked toward the lake where she'd given herself to Henry. His sweet whispered words of love, of wanting her to wait for him, that as soon as he procured enough funds to support his Scottish estate they would marry, flittered through her mind. What a liar he'd turned out to be. All he wanted was her innocence and nothing else.

Anger thrummed through her and she grit her teeth. How dare Henry trick her in such a way? Made her fall in love with him, promised to be faithful and marry her when he returned. He never wished to marry her. Had he wanted to right now he would be on his way back to England.

She turned, staring at her parents who looked resigned to a fate none of them imagined possible or ever wanted. "I will marry Viscount Newland. Write them and organize the nuptials to take place within the month or sooner if possible. The child I carry needs a father and the viscount needs a wife."

"Then it is done." Her father stood, walking over to her and taking her hand. "Did Henry promise you anything, Elizabeth? The letter is so out of character for him, I've wondered since receiving it that it isn't really of his opinion but his uncle's only."

"He wanted me to wait for him, to give him time to save his family's estate. He did not wish to marry a woman for her money; he wanted to be a self-made man, I suppose."

"Lies, Elizabeth. All lies," her mother stated, her voice cold. "Henry has used you, I fear, and I highly doubt he'll ever come back to England or Scotland, for that matter."

Elizabeth swallowed the lump in her throat, not wanting to believe the man she'd given her heart to would treat her in such a way. She'd thought Henry was different, was a gentleman who loved her. At the look of pity her father bestowed on her, she pushed him aside and ran from the room.

She needed air, fresh, cooling, calming air. Opening the front door, the chilling icy wind hit her face, and clarity assailed. She'd go for a ride. Her mount Argo always made her feel better.

It took the stable hand only minutes to saddle her mount, and she was soon trotting away from the house, the only sound that of the snow crunching beneath her horse's hooves. The chill pierced through her gown, and she regretted not changing into a suitable habit, but riding astride in whatever they had on at the time was a normal practice for the children of the Duke of Penworth. Too much freedom as a child, all of them allowed to do whatever they pleased, and now that freedom had led her straight into the worst type of trouble.

She pushed her horse into a slow canter, her mind a kaleidoscope of turmoil. Henry, once her father's ward, a person she'd thought to call a friend, had betrayed her when she needed him most. Guilt and shame swamped her just as snow started to fall, and covered everything in a crystal white hue.

She would never forgive Henry for this. Yes, they'd made a mistake, a terrible lack of decorum on her behalf that she'd never had time to think through. But should the worst happen, a child, she had consoled herself that Henry would do right by her, return home and marry her.

How could she have been so wrong?

She clutched her stomach, still no signs that a little child grew inside, and as much as she was ruined, could possibly ruin her family, she didn't regret her condition, and nor would she birth this child out of wedlock. Lord Newland would marry her since his situation was not looked upon favorably by the ton; it was a match that would suit them both.

Guilt pricked her soul that she would pass off Henry's child as Lord Newland's, but what choice did she have? Henry would not marry her, declare the child his. Elizabeth had little choice. There was nothing else to be done about it.

A deer shot out of the bracken, and Argo shied, jumping

sharply to the side. Elizabeth screamed as her seat slipped. The action unbalanced her and she fell, hitting the ground hard.

Luckily, the soft snow buffered her fall, and she sat up, feeling the same as she had when upon her horse. She rubbed her stomach, tears pooling in her eyes with the thought that had she fallen harder, all her problems would be over. What a terrible person she was to think such a thing, and how she hated Henry that his refusal of her had brought such horrendous thoughts to mind.

Argo nuzzled her side as she stood; reaching for the stirrup, she hoisted herself back onto her mount. Wiping the tears from her eyes, Elizabeth promised no more would be shed over a boy, for that was surely what Henry still was, an immature youth who gave no thought to others.

She would marry Viscount Newland, try and make him happy as much as possible when two strangers came together in such a union, and be damned anyone who mentioned the name Henry Andrews, Lord Muir to her again.

America 1805 – New York Harbor

*H*enry raised his face to the wind and rain as the packet ship sailed up the Hudson River. The damp winter air matched the cold he felt inside, numbing the pain that hadn't left his core since farewelling the shores of England. And now he was here. America. The smoky city just waking to a new day looked close enough to reach out and touch, and yet his true love, Elizabeth, was farther away than she'd ever been before.

He rubbed his chest and huddled into his greatcoat. The

five weeks across the ocean had dragged, endless days with his mind occupied with only one thought: his Elizabeth lass.

He shut his eyes, bringing the vision of her to his mind, her honest, laughing gaze, the beautiful smile that had always managed to make his breath catch. He frowned, missing her as much as the highland night sky would miss the stars.

"So, Henry, lad, what's your plan on these great lands?" Henry took in the captain on the British Government packet; his graying whiskers across his jaw and crinkled skin about his eyes told of a man who'd lived at sea his entire life, and enjoyed every moment of it. He grinned. "Make me fortune. Mend a broken family tie if I can."

The captain lit a cheroot and puffed, the smoke soon lost in the misty air. "Ah, grand plans then. Any ideas on how you'll be making your fortune? I could use some tips myself."

"My uncle lives here. Owns a shipping company apparently, although I've yet to meet the man or see for myself if this is true. I'm hoping since he's done so well for himself he can steer me along the road to me own fortune."

The captain nodded, staring toward the bow. "It seems you have it all covered."

Henry started when the captain yelled orders for half-mast. He hoped the old man was right with his statement. The less time he stayed here the better it would be. He pushed away the thought that Elizabeth was due to come out in the forthcoming months, to be paraded around the ton like a delicious morsel of sweet meats. To be the center of attention, a duke's daughter ripe for the picking. He ground his teeth.

"I wish you good luck, Henry."

"Thank ye." The captain moved away, and he turned back to look at the city so unlike London or his highland home. Foreign and wrong on so many levels. The muddy waters were the only similarity to London, he mused, smiling a little.

Henry walked to the bow, leaning over the wooden rail. He sighed, trying to expel the sullen mood that had swamped him the closer they came to America. What he was doing here was a good thing, an honorable thing, something that if he didn't do, Elizabeth would be lost to him forever.

He couldn't have hated his grandfather more at that moment for having lost their fortune at the turn of a card all those years ago. It was a miracle his father had been able to keep Avonmore afloat and himself out of debtor's prison.

The crewmen preparing the packet ship for docking sounded around him, and he started toward the small room he'd been afforded for the duration of the trip. It was better than nothing; even if he'd not been able to stand up fully within the space, at least it was private and comfortable.

Determination to succeed, to ensure his and Elizabeth's future was secure, to return home as soon as he may, sparked within him. He would not fail; for once, the Earl of Muir would not gamble the estate's future away, but fight for its survival, earn it respectably just as his ancestors had.

And he would return home, marry his English lass, and spoil her for the remainder of their days. In Scotland.

Want to read more? Purchase Only an Earl Will Do today!

LORDS OF LONDON SERIES AVAILABLE NOW!

Dive into these charming historical romances! In this six-book series by Tamara Gill, Darcy seduces a virginal duke, Cecilia's world collides with a roguish marquess, Katherine strikes a deal with an unlucky earl and Lizzy sets out to conquer a very wicked Viscount. These stories plus more adventures in the Lords of London series!

Lords of London

LEAGUE OF UNWEDDABLE GENTLEMEN SERIES AVAILABLE NOW!

Fall into my latest series, where the heroines have to fight for what they want, both regarding their life and love. And where the heroes may be unweddable to begin with, that is until they meet the women who'll change their fate. The League of Unweddable Gentlemen series is available now!

LEAGUE OF UNWEDDABLE GENTLEMEN

THE ROYAL HOUSE OF ATHARIA SERIES

If you love dashing dukes and want a royal adventure, make sure to check out my latest series, The Royal House of Atharia series! Book one, To Dream of You is available now at Amazon or you can read FREE with Kindle Unlimited.

A union between a princess and a lowly future duke is forbidden. But as intrigue abounds and their enemies circle, will Drew and Holly defy the obligations and expectations that stand between them to take a chance on love? Or is their happily ever after merely a dream?

ALSO BY TAMARA GILL

Royal House of Atharia Series
TO DREAM OF YOU
A ROYAL PROPOSITION
FOREVER MY PRINCESS

League of Unweddable Gentlemen Series
TEMPT ME, YOUR GRACE
HELLION AT HEART
DARE TO BE SCANDALOUS
TO BE WICKED WITH YOU
KISS ME DUKE
THE MARQUESS IS MINE
LEAGUE - BOOKS 1-3 BUNDLE
LEAGUE - BOOKS 4-6 BUNDLE

Kiss the Wallflower series
A MIDSUMMER KISS
A KISS AT MISTLETOE
A KISS IN SPRING
TO FALL FOR A KISS
A DUKE'S WILD KISS
TO KISS A HIGHLAND ROSE
KISS THE WALLFLOWER - BOOKS 1-3 BUNDLE
KISS THE WALLFLOWER - BOOKS 4-6 BUNDLE

Lords of London Series

TO BEDEVIL A DUKE
TO MADDEN A MARQUESS
TO TEMPT AN EARL
TO VEX A VISCOUNT
TO DARE A DUCHESS
TO MARRY A MARCHIONESS
LORDS OF LONDON - BOOKS 1-3 BUNDLE
LORDS OF LONDON - BOOKS 4-6 BUNDLE

To Marry a Rogue Series
ONLY AN EARL WILL DO
ONLY A DUKE WILL DO
ONLY A VISCOUNT WILL DO
ONLY A MARQUESS WILL DO
ONLY A LADY WILL DO

A Time Traveler's Highland Love Series
TO CONQUER A SCOT
TO SAVE A SAVAGE SCOT
TO WIN A HIGHLAND SCOT

Time Travel Romance
DEFIANT SURRENDER
A STOLEN SEASON

Scandalous London Series
A GENTLEMAN'S PROMISE
A CAPTAIN'S ORDER
A MARRIAGE MADE IN MAYFAIR
SCANDALOUS LONDON - BOOKS 1-3 BUNDLE

High Seas & High Stakes Series
HIS LADY SMUGGLER
HER GENTLEMAN PIRATE
HIGH SEAS & HIGH STAKES - BOOKS 1-2 BUNDLE

Daughters Of The Gods Series
BANISHED-GUARDIAN-FALLEN
DAUGHTERS OF THE GODS - BOOKS 1-3 BUNDLE

Stand Alone Books
TO SIN WITH SCANDAL
OUTLAWS

ABOUT THE AUTHOR

Tamara is an Australian author who grew up in an old mining town in country South Australia, where her love of history was founded. So much so, she made her darling husband travel to the UK for their honeymoon, where she dragged him from one historical monument and castle to another.

A mother of three, her two little gentlemen in the making, a future lady (she hopes) and a part-time job keep her busy in the real world, but whenever she gets a moment's peace she loves to write romance novels in an array of genres, including regency, medieval and time travel.

www.tamaragill.com
tamaragillauthor@gmail.com

Made in the USA
Columbia, SC
05 December 2021